PEACE

PEACE

RICHARD BAUSCH

Tuskar Rock
LONDON

First published in the United States of America in 2008
by Alfred A. Knopf, a division of Random House, Inc.

First published in hardback in Great Britain in 2009
by Tuskar Rock Press, an imprint of Grove Atlantic Ltd.

1 3 5 7 9 10 8 6 4 2

A CIP catalogue record for this book is available from
the British Library.

978 1 84887 084 0

Printed in Great Britain

Atlantic Books
An imprint of Grove Atlantic Ltd
Ormond House
26–27 Boswell Street
London WC1N 3JZ

www.atlantic-books.co.uk

With love, for

ANN MARIE BAUSCH *and* WESLEY BAUSCH,

who read these pages first

And in loving memory of my father,

ROBERT CARL BAUSCH,

who served bravely in Africa, Sicily, and Italy

Lo, the moon ascending,
Up from the east the silvery round moon,
Beautiful . . .

And my heart, O my soldiers, my veterans,
My heart gives you love.

—WALT WHITMAN
"Dirge for Two Veterans," *Drum Taps*

With deepest gratitude, love, and admiration to George Garrett,
who for almost twenty years kept after me to write this story

PEACE

ONE

THEY WENT ON ANYWAY, putting one foot in front of the other, holding their carbines barrel down to keep the water out, trying, in their misery and confusion—and their exhaustion—to remain watchful. This was the fourth straight day of rain—a windless, freezing downpour without any slight variation of itself. Rivulets of ice formed in the muck of the road and made the walking treacherous. The muscles of their legs burned and shuddered, and none of them could get enough air. Robert Marson thought about how they were all witnesses. And nobody could look anybody in the eye. They kept on, and were punished as they went. Ice glazed their helmets, stuck to the collars of their field jackets, and the rain got in everywhere, soaking them to the bone. They were somewhere near Cassino, but it was hard to believe it was even Italy anymore. They had stumbled blind into some province of drenching cold, a berg of death. Everything was in question now.

3

The Italians had quit, and the Germans were retreating, engaging in delaying actions, giving way slowly, skirmishing, seeking to make every inch of ground costly in time and in blood, and there were reconnaissance patrols all along the front, pushing north, heading into the uncertainty of where the Germans might be running, or waiting.

Marson, sick to his soul, barely matched the pace of the two men just in front of him, who were new. Their names were Lockhart and McCaig, and they themselves lagged behind four others: Troutman, Asch, Joyner, and Sergeant Glick. Seven men. Six witnesses.

The orders had been to keep going until you found the enemy. Then you were supposed to make your way back, preferably without having been seen. But the enemy had the same kinds of patrols, and so recon also meant going forward until you were fired upon. Worse, this was a foot patrol. If you ran into anything serious, there wouldn't be any jeeps to ride out, nor tanks to help you. You were alone in the waste of the war.

And there were only the seven of them now.

Twelve men had left one tank battalion the first day, crossed country, and then slept under the tanks of another on the second, all in the changeless fall of the rain. McConnell, Padruc, and Bailey came down with the dysentery and had to be taken back to Naples. So the patrol left that camp with nine men.

Walberg and Hopewell were killed yesterday.

Yesterday, a farmer's cart full of wet straw had come strag-
gling along the road being pulled by a donkey and driven by
two Italian boys—gypsies, really—who looked like sopping
girls, their long, black, soaked hair framing their faces, their
wet cloaks hiding their bodies. Sergeant Glick waved them
away, and they melted into the glazed second growth beside
the road. Then he ordered that the cart be overturned in
order to look for weapons or contraband. Troutman and Asch
accomplished this, and as the waterlogged, mud-darkened
straw collapsed from the bed of the cart, a Kraut officer and a
whore tumbled out, cursing. The Kraut shot Walberg and
Hopewell with his black Luger before Corporal Marson put
him down. The whore, soggy and dirty and ill looking, wear-
ing another officer's tunic over a brown skirt, spoke only German, and she shouted more curses at them, gesticulating and
trying to hit at McCaig and Joyner, who held her. Sergeant
Glick looked at Hopewell and Walberg, ascertained that they
were dead, then walked over, put the end of his carbine at her
forehead, and fired. The shot stopped the sound of her. She
fell back into the tall wet stalks of grass by the side of the road,
so that only her lower legs and her feet showed. She went over
backward; the legs came up and then dropped with a thud
into the sudden silence. Marson, who had been looking at the
Kraut he shot, heard the fourth shot and turned to see this.
And he saw the curve of her calves, the feet in a man's boots
where they jutted from the grass. For a few seconds, no one
said anything. They all stood silent and did not look at one
another, or at Glick, and the only sound was the rain.

"She was with him. She'd've shot us all if she could," Glick said. No one answered him. Marson had shot the Kraut, and he was having trouble with that, and here were the woman's legs stuck out of the grass next to the road. The curve of the calves was that of a young woman. "This is all one thing," Glick said, loud. It was as if he were talking to the earth and sky. The others knew he meant that the woman had been a reaction, two men killed like that—shot, both of them, through the heart—completely unready for it, though Glick had repeatedly told them and they all knew that they should be ready, every second, for just this. This. Walberg and Hopewell, two boys. Hopewell had just been talking about being at a restaurant in Miami Beach, eating Dungeness crabs, how much he wished he were there right now. And Walberg, quiet Walberg, only this morning had been going on about his father, who was a hero to him, and the others had been embarrassed hearing him describe the old man, because of the childlike devotion in it, the hero worship. "Grow up, Walberg," Asch had said once. And Walberg had grown up to this, lying by the side of a road somewhere near Cassino, with an expression on his face of mild surprise. Hopewell's eyes were closed. He looked like he was asleep.

And they had all been warned to be ready, every second.

But it had been so cold, and the rain kept coming down on them. They had got numb, maybe even drowsy—the drowse before you lie down and freeze to death. And they couldn't really look at one another now, and still nobody looked at Glick.

Because this was a recon squad—and because the Germans had taken over everything, the war and the retreat and the defense of Italy, and could be close—they had to leave Walberg and Hopewell beside the road and move on, away from the scene, while light left the low, charred-looking folds of the sky. Troutman had radioed back.

There had followed an abysmal long night without any respite from the cold and the rain. Through it all, nobody spoke of what had taken place back down the road. But Marson kept feeling the sickness. It was as if something in him had been leveled, and the simplest memories of himself as he had always been were beside the point. He was devout, because his people were devout, and because it was a strength, and he kept trying to pray, kept saying the words in his mind. *All for thee, most sacred heart of Jesus.* An offering, as he had been taught. Expiation for his sins, for everything he had ever done that was wrong. It meant little, now. At times he would speak directly to God in his mind, like a man talking to another man—except that it was somehow more than one other man or, really, one god, but something nameless and immense beyond the raining sky: *Let me get through this, help me find forgiveness, and I'll raise a big family.* He had a daughter back home, a thirteen-month-old girl whom he had yet to see in person. He kept her photograph tucked away under his shirt, in a flat cigarette tin.

He could not let himself think very much at all. The others were quiet, sullen, isolated. And yet after the misery of the fitful night, they seemed to have put it in its place. It was the war; it was what they had been through. They had lived with confusion for so long. Nobody said anything about it.

They just slogged on, always north. And the sickness kept coming over Marson in waves. He had been on the beachhead at Salerno. His company had been pinned down for hours leading into days, and he had lived through the panic when all along the line men believed that the enemy had infiltrated the ranks, and they froze on their weapons and shot members of their own outfit who had gone beyond them. He had fired mortar rounds into the roil and tumult of the fortifications beyond the beach, had been in the fighting all the way to Persano and the Sele River, and he knew intellectually that he had certainly killed several men.

He had seen so much death, and the dead no longer caused quite the same shock. Not even poor Walberg and Hopewell. He had experienced that kind of sudden stop before now. But he hadn't, himself, until yesterday, killed anyone up close. The Kraut had a big round boy's face and bright red hair, and the bullet had gone into him just above the breastbone and exited with a blast of blood and flesh out the back of his neck, into the distance behind him. He coughed bright blood mixed with something he must've had to eat, looking right at Corporal Marson with an expression terrifyingly like wonder, while the light or the animation or whatever it was left his green eyes, and the eyes started to reflect the raining sky, the clear, icy water gathering in them and running down the white face.

TWO

Sunny Italy, John Glick had been calling it, spitting the words out, the standard joke in the lines. He was from New York and had worked as a longshoreman for a year out of high school, and you could hear it in his voice.

Four straight days of rain. It felt like the end of the world. The North Atlantic had gone up into the sky and traveled south and was coming down with temperatures wavering at the freezing point.

At early dusk today, another tank battalion caught up with them. They got under the tanks and ate rations, coughing and sputtering. Glick went a few paces down the row of tanks and half-tracks and reported about Walberg and Hopewell, the Kraut and the woman. Marson heard him say that she had been killed in the cross fire. He saw Joyner hear it, too, and Joyner looked at him, but then looked away. Nobody else in this battalion had run into any action yesterday, though

Marson, crossing to the far side of the range of tanks and other equipment, encountered a soldier they had all talked to several days before, and he was sitting in the back of a jeep, holding his hand and crying. The hand had been burned badly; it was black and two of the fingers looked like charred twigs, and it was shaking as with a palsy. The soldier kept staring at it, crying like a little kid. No one could talk to him.

Marson gave forth a little sobbing breath, and turned away.

It was for what was called his steadiness on the beachhead at Salerno that he had been given a field promotion to corporal. The promoting officer used the word. Marson's company had been held down by machine-gun fire, and he had bolted forward to a shell crater in the sand and then lobbed grenades at the emplacement. Others had followed him, and the enemy withdrew, abandoning their own machine gun. There had been no time to think and in his memory of it, it was like trying to stop a leak in a seawall, shouting all the time. Marson had felt no steadiness, but only the sense of trying very hard not to die, and the frozen conviction at his middle that he would not survive the next minute. He was older than most of these boys, twenty-six. It astonished him that so many of them believed that they could not die. Even seeing death on the beach at Salerno.

Now he and Joyner sat in a mired jeep briefly to get out of the rain. They did not particularly like each other. There had been tension between them before. Joyner had a set of attitudes about Negroes, Jews, and Catholics, and his assertions, along with the obscenity of his speech in general, had an unpleasant air of authority about them, as if he had done serious study and come to serious conclusions. But it all came from ignorance and bigotry. Joyner, apparently sensing the effect on Marson, claimed he was joking. But for Marson the jokes were seldom very clever, or very funny, and it was unnerving. He had, to his great discomfort, discerned the thinnest echo of his own casually held assumptions in the other man's talk. And so he had worked to keep a distance.

Until now.

He had seen the look Joyner gave him when Sergeant Glick spoke of the whore's death. So, sitting behind the driver's wheel of the jeep, he had the sense that he ought to see if Joyner, given the chance, might say something. Except that he was too honest with himself to believe this was the only motive: the truth was that he wanted to learn what all the others felt. He was too muddled and tired to think clearly enough. But he wanted to know.

Joyner did not disappoint him. Watching him light a cigarette and blow the smoke, he muttered: "Some cross fire, huh?"

Marson looked over at him and then looked away. It came to him that he did not want to talk about it with Joyner. Not with him.

"Cross fire like that and you don't need a fuck'n firing squad," Joyner went on, smiling, spitting from between his teeth, a habit he had. He was tall and narrow eyed, with a long nose and big, wide-fingered hands that always shook. He had once talked of how it was a problem lighting a lady's cigarette. And he had sworn it wasn't nerves. He had a recurring itch on his left forearm. That, he said, *was* nerves, since he'd never had anything like it until the war. It was always there, since Sicily, and he kept having to dig at it.

They sat together in the front seat of the jeep, which was up to its axle in the mud of the road and was therefore out of the war for now. They did not quite look at each other. Marson drew on the cigarette.

"I thought Salerno was fucked up," Joyner said, scratching the place on his forearm.

At Salerno, he had been entrenched with several others near a crippled LCI that rolled back and forth in the heavy waves behind them. They heard the loud pinging of bullets hitting the metal of the LCI, and Joyner kept up a stream of obscenities. It made a strange undersound to the crackle of the firing and the waves pounding, the planes going over and the bombs falling, and the high whistle of the ordnance coming from the ships at the horizon line, and the screams of those who had been hit. Finally he broke from the trench and came running. He crossed a wide rib of sand and ossified wood and dropped down next to a corpsman, who fell in the next instant, helmet breaking with the metal clank of the bullet or fragment that killed him. Joyner fired at the culvert above them and kept firing. Then he screamed. "Fuck!" It went off in a falsetto shriek. And that was when the realization came to them all that the firing from the culvert had all but ceased.

They rushed it, and overran it, and found that after days of delivering a withering fire, the enemy had withdrawn. Joyner sat against the seawall and wept like a baby, mouth agape, eyes closed, the tears running.

Now, sitting with him in the jeep in the pelting rain, smoking the cigarette, the corporal remembered this pass and kept his eyes averted.

"I don't give a shit about it," Joyner said suddenly. "You know that, right?"

Marson offered him a drag of the cigarette.

"Fuck you."

"Just trying to keep the peace, there, Joyner."

"Yeah. Peace. Would you have tried to stop it?"

"I didn't see it happen. I heard it and looked."

"That isn't what I asked you."

"The answer is, I don't know. Okay? There wasn't a vote, you know. I don't think anybody could've done anything."

"You're white as a sheet."

Marson took a drag of the cigarette and did not answer. They were quiet for a little while.

"You look like all hell."

"What would you have done?" Marson asked him. "Would you have tried to stop it?"

"Fuck," Joyner said. "I'd've shot her myself. But I wouldn't have called it a fuck'n cross fire."

Marson felt the sickness. But he could not tell this to Joyner or show it to him.

"This rain is the fuck'n end-times," Joyner said abruptly. "The end of the fuck'n world."

"It's rain," said the corporal.

"I'm telling you I never saw four straight goddamn days of fuck'n ice falling from the fuck'n sky."

Sergeant Glick came back past the line of tanks. "Fall in," he said. He'd been given five new troops. He ordered them to say their names. They stood on either side of him, like the members of a posse. They looked weary and aggravated, muttering their own names. Phillips, Carrick, Dorfman, Bruce, Nyman.

"The Jerries are still rolling back," Glick said. "But they're leaving stragglers, for attrition. You all get that?"

The men made a general low sound of agreement.

"There's snipers and combat patrols out there, looking to make us miserable."

"Mission already accomplished," said Asch. A couple of the new men laughed.

"If you don't want to die," Glick said, "you'll keep your eyes peeled and your weapons ready and your ears open."

"Got a back problem, Sergeant," Asch said.

"Should've had it looked at Stateside," Glick said. But he knew what was coming.

"Nobody would do a thing about it."

"That's tough."

"Yeah, Sarge."

"Cut it out, Asch."

"Yeah, trouble is, I got a big wide yellow streak right down the middle of it."

"Asch, I might have you court-martialed just for your mouth."

"Watch for those snipers, Sarge."

THREE

THEY ALL HEADED OUT, still north, still on foot. The road was deep mud, turning to ice, grabbing at their feet, and the rain kept coming—straight down, relentless, pitiless, miserable. At some point during today's march, Marson had developed a blister on his right heel. Some inconsistency or tear in the leather of the insole in his boot hurt him with each step, and each step made it worse, and the sickness was still with him.

The pain went up to his ankle, shooting, like nerve pain. There wasn't any way to favor it. Even limping seemed to give no relief. And each time the images of what happened on the road came to him—Walberg and Hopewell lying so still; the woman's legs jutting from the grass; the green eyes of the soldier he had shot, reflecting light, the look of wonder in the white face—each time these things went through him, his gorge rose. But then, in the freezing minutes turning into hours that went on, and on, he found himself realizing that this shock, like all the others, was fading, too. And there was just the constant, hollow presence of the nausea, along with the searing pain in his heel. Everyone was suffering a kind of low-grade shock, aware of the badness of being here, out of all the places there were to be in the world.

You marched into the tide of the war and arrived nowhere. Or you were among those who gave way to the lure of the war and rode off with a company of fools, looking for trouble. Asch trudged along next to him, muttering about the inadequacy of the army's version of a field jacket to keep out the rain and the cold. But then he leaned toward Marson and said, "We gotta do something."

Marson looked over at him, but said nothing.

"What are we, anyway?"

"Are you asking me?" Marson said.

Glick, a few yards ahead of them, turned and barked at a couple of the new troops: "Keep your distance, somebody'll get you both with one shot."

Asch dropped back a pace or two and moved to the right. He said, "My uncle's a police officer."

Marson glanced over at him.

"Homicide detective."

"Really."

"Twenty years."

Marson tried to adjust his stride to accommodate the pain in his heel and ankle. It was only getting worse.

"Do you ever wonder how somebody can do that all those years? One murder after another?"

"Never gave it any thought," Marson said.

"I never did, either, I guess. Until now."

Marson looked at him. "I know," he said. "It's a thought."

"Lot of them unsolved, too. Used to be kind of frustrating to him. The one thing he really hated was the people who could've helped him and wouldn't."

"Guess that would be hard."

"People who saw things and wouldn't say what they saw."

"Right."

"Yeah," Asch said. "Right."

"Did he ever figure what to do about it?"

"No."

"He still on the force?"

"Twenty years," Asch said.

Marson looked over at him. Asch was staring, his helmet pushed back, the rain splattering his face.

"You know what I mean?"

"That's a lot of years," Marson said.

"A lot of murders," said Asch.

Marson did not answer him this time. He experienced the nausea and the cold, and ahead of him the others were mechanically going on, shoulders hunched, the rain beating down on them, thin, falling strands of ice.

When they stopped to rest for a few minutes in the shell of a farmhouse, he worked to get his boot off to try doing something about the foot. But it was the shape of the heel itself, something pushing upward from the insole, a wrinkle. The foot looked whiter than could be healthy, except for the place where the blister bulged. He broke it with the point of his bayonet and let it run, and the flap of skin, about the size of a quarter, collapsed into the redness, the inflamed center of the abrasion. It hurt to touch it. He let the rain pelt it as long as he could, until the sting was too much, and then he put the sock back on—it was wet through, and heavy—and the boot, hurting, trying to offer up the pain, trying to think in terms of the prayer. *All for thee.* The foot throbbed, and there was the problem of the cold now, too, and the marching went on, and each time he put the weight of himself on the foot, the pain shot up to his ankle, a piercing white-hot flash. He winced at it and went on, and suffered it. A flatness had settled into his spirit, a dead feeling at the heart. It was as if the physical pain could have been happening to someone else. It did not reach into him, quite. There was something removed at the very center, and he could turn in his mind and look at the empty place.

FOUR

Toward sundown, they stopped where a fast-moving river came up to the edge of the road on the left and went on, veering off again into the trees. The road wound sharply to the right and out of sight beyond the rise of a steep hill. There were trees on that side, too. Through the trees to the left was the water, metal gray and solid looking, with little quick flags of white in it. Now and again a tree branch came gliding past, and then they saw boards and other debris, followed by the legs of a horse, the animal being pulled along in the swirling eddies, bobbing in and out of the folds of water, the legs frozen in an attitude of flight. The river churned and roared. They all moved to the right of the road and the base of the hill, where the wet black branches provided some meager shelter. All the trees were beginning to look as though they were made of glass. There were tank tracks in the mud and stones of the road. Glick had Troutman bring the radio to him and reported this, and they all waited. There wasn't any sound but the rain coming down. The word came through to keep going.

But Glick didn't move. The others watched him. Little slivers of ice dropped down off his helmet. It took another moment for them to realize that he had seen something coming from the bend of the road. It was another farm cart, this one being pulled by a horse. A crooked shape in brown, a hooded man with dark thin hands, held the reins. Under the hood was only the suggestion of a gaunt face in shadow. The cart came abreast of them, and Glick rushed it, his carbine at the ready. The figure stopped the cart and stood in it, hands up. It was an old man. He looked at them wide eyed and spoke in a trembling reedy voice. "*Sono italiano.* Speaka English." Then in Italian again: "*Non sono tedesco! Amico, sono il vostro amico. Amico. Non uccidermi! Non spararmi! Per favore!* No shoot."

"You *capeesh* English?" Glick said to him.

"*Poco,*" the old man said through a wide grimace that showed broken and decayed teeth. "*Sì, un po'.* Little. Speaka the English. Little. *Sì.*"

"Get down off the cart."

He hesitated, looking at them all, plainly unsure of what was being asked and fearing that any miscalculation would be the end of him. Then: "*Cedo! Non spararmi!* Surrender! No shoot, *per favore.*"

"Down," Glick said, gesturing. "Get the fuck down."

The rain on the old man's lined, bony face made it look as

though he was crying. His eyes were squeezed tight, the brows pinched. It was a look of great sorrow. Glick motioned with the end of the rifle. "Now," he said. And with alacrity, evidently trying desperately to please, the old man climbed down.

Glick got Lockhart to unhitch the horse and then ordered Joyner and Troutman to upset the cart while the others crouched, ready to fire. He instructed Marson to cover the old man, who stood there quietly with the rain beating down on him, the cowl-like hood obscuring much of his face. The cloak he wore was made of the same canvas material that was stretched over whatever was in the cart. He wore rope-soled shoes, and his pants were thick burlap, drooping past the ankles, mud stained and wet to the knees. The look of him was of a kind of sad resignation—here was his cart, with all his belongings in it, being overturned in the road. The cart contained nothing but the possessions of somebody trying to ride with his little life away from a war. Marson thought of the old man's humiliation: shoes and dishes and pictures of family members, clothes, books, cooking utensils. The old man turned away slightly, as if the sight of these things hurt him.

"You know this country?" Glick asked him, "*Capeesh?*" He made a motion to include the trees and the tall hill, the sodden surroundings.

"*Sì, sì.*"

"Guide? Scout?" Glick turned and pointed up the hill into the trees.

"Scout." The man simply repeated the word.

Glick pointed at the bend in the road. "German?"

The old man nodded, but it was impossible to tell whether he meant that he understood or that there were Jerries up the road. He stood there with that look of resignation and watched the rain collect in the little folds of his thrown clothing and on his belongings lying in the mud.

"Set the cart right," Glick told the others. "Put his stuff back. Marson, keep your rifle on him."

The others did as they were told. For Marson, it felt for a moment all right, even with the general terror, the pain, and the shivering. It was a correction. The old man watched them.

"You guide?" Glick said, pointing up into the trees.

The man stared at him.

"Go up over fucking hill," Glick said with exaggerated slowness, pointing. "Christ sakes. See fucking road. Get it? Over the fucking hill, see the fucking road."

Marson indicated himself, and then the old man, and then the hill rising behind him. "Guide," he said.

"Oh, *sì. Sì. Vi guiderò. Sì*, yes."

"*Guiderò.* Guide," Glick said.

"Yes. *Sì.*"

He turned to Marson. "Take Asch and Joyner."

The old man waited, turning slightly. The sergeant ordered the cart pulled off the road, into the trees by the river. The horse had been tied to one of the trees there, and it stood watching them all, blinking in the rain but apparently not even quite noticing it, tearing at the grass at the base of the tree and chewing, staring. The blanket over its haunches had gone black with soaking, and it gave off a stream of little silver turning-to-ice drops.

"Now," Glick said. "Goddamn. What're you waiting for? Move it."

The old man nodded, then turned to Marson and motioned for him to follow. Marson thought he saw something of a smile on the wet, drawn, aged features. A look of relief, he realized.

"Asch," he said. "Joyner."

The two troops fell in line and they started up into the trees, the old man leading the way.

FIVE

IT WAS SLOW GOING. The hill became steadily steeper, and it was slippery. A thick bed of pine needles and mud and dead leaves covered the ground. They had to dig with the toes of their boots to make footholds in it. They hadn't gone fifty yards before Asch fell and slipped back, and he made a sound like a yelp, an animal noise. He had hit the trunk of a tree on the way down. He had been stopped by it.

Marson, Joyner, and the old man waited for him to get up. They were still in sight of the others on the road, who were now resting in the failing light, huddled in the torrent, the relentless emptying sky.

"Christ, why us?" Joyner said, to no one in particular.

They waited, and Asch fell again, cursing.

"Shit sakes, Asch," Joyner said.

The old man had paused, one leg up, ready to keep on, and his face was impassive, merely interested in Asch's progress climbing back to them. At one point, Asch went to his knees and stayed there, his face contorted with the effort and with the frustration of not being able to gain his footing. But then his expression changed. He sighed and leaned forward and rested his arms on the barrel of his carbine. He seemed almost content, kneeling there while they gazed down at him, perhaps twenty yards farther up.

"Come on, asshole," Joyner said.

"Fuck you," said Asch.

Marson thought he heard Joyner say something under his breath. He believed he had heard the word *Yid*. He looked at Joyner, who had pulled a rag out of his field jacket and was wiping his face.

"You'd best keep your opinions to yourself," he said.

Joyner folded the rag and put it away and then merely stared.

"Got it?" Marson said.

"I *capeesh*," said Joyner. "What're you gonna do, fire me?"

Asch got to them and then dropped to his knees again, having slipped and stopped himself. He turned and looked back down at the road. "I'm shorter than you guys. It's harder to climb. Don't go so fast."

"We don't have all night," the corporal said.

"You think they're above us? Waiting up there?" Asch wanted to know.

"How the fuck would we have that information," said Joyner.

"Just keep alert," Marson told them.

"Going down this fucker isn't going to be much easier than going up if we have to move quick," Asch said. "I really hit my back on that sapling going down. Can we take a minute? It really hurts."

"Maybe you should head on back down, darling," Joyner said. "We wouldn't want you to get a boo-boo."

"Fuck yourself," Asch told him. "Better yet, why don't you stand up real straight, and then fall through your asshole and hang yourself?"

"Bright boy," Joyner said. "All you New York guys are so bright."

"Shut up," Marson said.

"All of *what* guys, Joyner. You want to give me a more specific category? I happen to be from Boston."

"You know what category."

"I don't have any idea, buddy. Why don't you fill me in?"

Joyner said nothing.

The old man stood there watching them with that expression of calm interest. When he saw Corporal Marson looking at him, he straightened slightly and pulled his own cloak higher around his neck.

"We're going to make this walk to the top of this hill and see what we can see," Marson said. "And then we're going to turn around and come back down, and we are not going to waste any energy fighting with each other. Got it?"

"I fell," Asch said. "Jesus. Tell him to lay off."

"No, I'm not getting between you. I'm telling you both how it's gonna be."

"You want to tell him to lay off the New York stuff? Because that's not what he means."

Marson looked at Joyner, who had a challenge in his eyes. The rain was making him blink, but his eyes were cold and defiant. "You didn't mean that like it sounded, right, Joyner?"

"Could've been talking about any big city," Joyner said.

"Fuck you," said Asch. "No matter what you were talking about."

The old man murmured something low.

"No *capeesh,*" Joyner said to him. "Did you say you want us to die choking on our own blood?"

The old man simply returned his gaze.

"This is a fuck'n Fascist, I'm telling you," Joyner said.

"*Non sono fascista,*" said the old man, with an earnest shaking of his head. He began to wring his old hands. It looked like he was trying to bend the bones in them.

"Now you've spooked him," Marson said. "Keep your mouth shut, Joyner. Just don't open it again."

Asch got to his feet. "I'm ready when you are," he said to Marson.

They turned and started up, following the path where the old man led them, still struggling with the steep angle of the hill and the slippery surface, with its little rushing trickles of water, the rain still beating down with the same windless fall.

"Oh, Christ," Joyner said. "Why does it have to be us?"

SIX

JOYNER WAS FROM MICHIGAN, a sheep farm there, where his father and grandfather and great-grandfather had lived; and his father had raised him to take over, in time. The war was his escape, as he had told anyone who would listen in the first days they all were together. He hated the farm—hated the *idea* of farming—and spent much of his time in high school following the good orchestras around the upper Midwest. He played clarinet, and his father thought of him as a bum, he said, and that was a tough thing to live with sometimes. He had once seen Benny Goodman at the Aragon Ballroom in Chicago, and he talked about the women he met that night and about walking along the lake in the summer dark with the city shining on the water. He could be expressive in that way, too, which made him all the more troublesome to Marson, who was himself expressive and liked what his mother always called *picture speech,* words and phrases that took you somewhere other than where you were. Joyner said that he liked Benny Goodman best because his own name was Benny, and then he went on to say that a coincidence of naming was no reason to like a man's music, either. But there it was.

And there Joyner was. He could talk about the moon shining on water, and yet obscenity flowed from him like the little beads of spit he kept throwing off. He would spray it out from between his teeth. This punctuated his talk, like a nerve-tic.

In Palermo, in training, he would look up and see Marson coming, and, knowing of Marson's reluctance to use bad language, he would spit and say, "Aw fuck-shit. I mean gosh." Others found it funny, including Asch, but it made Marson feel singled out.

"I got off the fuck'n farm and here I am in farm country, in fuck'n Italy," Joyner would say. It was as though he were reciting it.

"You should've brought your clarinet," Marson told him once, trying not to show how awkward he felt. He had been a Benny Goodman fan, too, though he liked Glenn Miller better. He tried to shift the subject to music.

But Joyner brought it back to Marson's devoutness. "No atheists in the foxholes, right, Marson?"

"I guess not," Marson said.

"Fuck a duck, huh?"

And it was Asch who laughed. "Joyner, you should be on Broadway."

"Nothing for me in Jew York, there, Asch."

"On the curbside on Broadway, darling."

"Yeah, that's me all right, in that town. I'd have to stay drunk all the time."

"Hey, I've got an idea, how about you kiss my ass?"

Like Marson, Joyner had been a star athlete in high school—right guard on the football team, forward on the basketball team. He played baseball, too, but wasn't as good at it, nor as interested in it. Marson had been so good at baseball that he played semipro for a couple of years. He had been around. He was the oldest man in the squad, two years older than Sergeant Glick. Joyner was only nineteen. He and Marson had come through training together. They were assigned to the division when it was still in Sicily, following the invasion there. Saul Asch had seen action in North Africa and he talked about a dream he kept having from a memory: a burning tank, the men in it, and the heat of the desert, the smell rising in the waves of black smoke and flames. He dreamed the smell, he said, and his tone was matter-of-fact, as though he were reporting some curiosity of the terrain. The dream did not appear to affect him. He was just twenty-three years old, with round little brown eyes and chubby boy's cheeks, the eldest of three brothers, all of whom were serving. He had barely made the height requirement. Marson had found him pleasurable to be around because of the way he had of turning everything into an observation, and there was the Boston accent. But he had lately been wanting to avoid him because of his talk about the recurring dream. It kept happening. "Had it again," he would say. "Same thing. The heat and the smell. Like I'm there again." He would shake his head and shrug. "You figure?" That was a phrase he used repeatedly to express puzzlement or wonder. He was Jewish, but, as he put it, never practiced. His grandfather was a German Jew who in his late thirties fought for the Kaiser in World War I. That always amazed him to think about. The grandfather had died last year in the living room of an apartment in Brockton, after eating a meal of salmon in dill sauce with his daughter-in-law, who had cooked the meal and came from Italy. That man had been in the other war, the first one, fighting on the other side. Asch talked about going from the Ardennes Forest, shooting at French and English and American soldiers, to a living room in Brockton—with a grandson about to join the army to go fight the Hun. It was ridiculous.

Marson possessed a strong sense of paradox, and he had liked this story. But he had been having trouble being around Asch: he would think of it, and of the Africa nightmare, every time Asch spoke. It was like backdrop. And now they had the woman's death between them, too.

Marson couldn't imagine Asch living long enough to be a grandfather. Probably it was the rounded cheeks, so boylike, so chubby and smooth. Marson couldn't look at him without thinking that the war would certainly kill him. But then, often he did not, himself, expect to survive it.

SEVEN

IT WAS ALMOST FULL DARK NOW. The cold was
a dead immensity on them. It was as though they were
moving through a film of ice, always climbing, weighted down
by web belt and pack, and the bandoliers and grenades, slip-
ping, fighting for air, following the old man, who seemed to
have grown younger as the distance between him and the
road increased. He climbed easily, and his breathing seemed
effortless. Marson watched him, his own lungs burning, his
legs trembling with the effort not to fall. The climb kept getting steeper, and he could hear his own heart pounding in his
ears. He gagged, and then gagged again, climbing. Each step
scraped the blister on his heel, and several times he had to use
the stock of his rifle like a cane, the palm of his hand over the
barrel opening, to support himself. Asch and Joyner were
silent, and they made no eye contact, automatically thrusting
themselves up with each step, using a tree branch now and

then to pull on. They came up, oblivious to anything but the slant of the ground where they were putting their boots—the rough angling upward of the earth with its rucks and broken branches and gouges of mud and leaf meal—and Marson kept looking back at them, checking their progress. It was too dark now to see where they were heading or where the hill might begin to crest or level off. There was just the endless climbing, pain deepening in the muscles of their legs and in their knees, the bones there. Because the ground was so steep, there didn't seem to be a way to rest without beginning the long slide back down. And all the while there was the unabating, remorseless, utter constancy of the rain.

The old man went on up, the incline so steep now that with each step that knee was close to his chest, the bony hand pushing on it, to gain the next increment of ground. Asch fell again and slid far enough to be out of sight. Joyner sat down and put the butt of his rifle against the ground between his feet, his field jacket sleeve across the barrel. He reached in under the sleeve and scratched the place on his forearm. Marson called softly to the old man. "Wait."

"*Sì.*"

The old man held on to the thin trunk of a tree, and Marson climbed to him, then turned. They could hear Asch struggling toward them from where he had fallen.

"*Che città* in America?" the old man said. "City you live?"

"Washington, D.C.," Marson said.

"I see Washington."

"Yeah?"

Silence. Just the clink of equipment on the belts, the rain beating their bodies and the helmets. Above them, the sky was inconsistently covering a full moon—there were thin places in it—but the rain kept beating down. The old man wiped the water from his chin and coughed. Then he bent a little at his knees, reached into his burlap trousers, and pulled out his prick. In the dimness, Marson saw the uncircumcised length of it. The old man urinated onto the soggy leaves at his feet. The urine steamed, running in thin tributaries away from him. He tucked himself back in and, looking at Marson, nodded slightly, with an embarrassed little smile.

"When did you see Washington?" Marson asked him.

After a hesitation, the old man nodded. "Younger. I travel. *Sono andato a* New York. I—I go to New York, too. Yes?"

"Yes," Marson told him. "I've never been."

The old man seemed mystified.

"No me," Marson said. "New York."

"Ah, *sì*."

"What is your name?"

Again the look.

"How are you called?"

The old man nodded. "Yes. *Sì*."

Marson pointed to himself. "Robert."

"*Sì*. Angelo."

"Angelo."

"Were you ever in the army, Angelo?"

"*Come?*"

Marson pointed to himself, his helmet with the water dripping from it. "Army. Military."

"Oh, *sì. Nella prima guerra.*"

"*Prima.* One. World War I."

"*Sì.*"

"Did you fight?"

The old man stared.

"Fight." Marson gestured, pantomimed shooting.

"*Sì. Ero un capitano.*"

Marson saluted him. "Captain, *sì*?"

The old man, Angelo, nodded. He had a hopeful expression on his face now. Water dripped from the creases of his hood and gathered at his chest, the large fold there. The rain got in. It ran searchingly down Marson's neck and into his blouse. He shivered. Asch made it to them, and finally they all headed up again, reaching for crevices and low branches because it was too steep to stand. The ground kept sliding beneath them, and the icy rain kept pelting their faces.

At last they came to a small area of level ground, and Marson said, "We'll rest here a little."

Angelo looked at him.

"Rest?" Marson said again.

"*Sì.*"

Asch and Joyner were already pulling their packs off. They set them down and, with their rifles across their thighs, squatted against an outcropping of rock, a ledge that channeled the rain away from them, down the mountain. It was a mountain. Marson realized that now. The old man moved to the ledge, to Asch's left. Marson joined him there. They were all four huddled in the lee of the rock, and the water ran on away from them, though Marson's knees were still exposed.

He took his blanket roll and opened it and held it over himself.

"Fuck," Asch said. "When I get out of this, I'm gonna live in the desert, I swear to Christ. I'm gonna move to Arizona. And if it rains *there* I'm moving. I'm gonna be somewhere in the sun." He sounded as though he might start shrieking.

"Keep it down," Marson told him. He almost choked on the words. The muscles of his abdomen contracted. He swallowed and took a slow breath. They were all quiet, hearing the noise of the rain that kept coming and coming.

"I'm telling you it's the end of the fucking world," Joyner said. "The world never had to deal with so much general destruction. How do we know we won't knock it right off its orbit into space?"

"Jesus, Ben. I got enough morbid shit running around in my head without worrying about *that,* too."

"Don't call me Ben. It's Benny."

"Sorry there, Joyner."

"Christ," Joyner said. "I never even got married." He put his hand in under his sleeve and scratched again.

"Wonder if my wife's had her baby," said Asch. Then, after clearing his throat: "I don't think a woman should die because she's got blood loyalty to a lover." He cleared his throat again, and bowed his head and spit. "Christ's sake."

"Saint Saul," Joyner said. "Maybe you didn't notice she was trying to claw my fuck'n eyes out."

"I noticed. I notice everything, buddy."

"Is that some kind of threat?"

"Shut up," Corporal Marson said. "Both of you."

Joyner turned to him. "You think anybody else is out in this shit, Marson?"

"If they are, and they're Jerries, they'll have weapons, too," Marson told him. "So shut it."

"I'm shivering so bad," Asch muttered. "I've got cramps from the shivering. I hit my back on a sapling, sliding down the fucking hill."

"It's not a hill," Joyner said, scratching. "It's a fuck'n mountain."

"Mountain, *sì*," said the old man. "*Montagna.*"

"This is bullshit, is what this is."

"Shut up," Corporal Marson said. "All of you."

They were quiet again. He looked out at the faintly glistening tree and branch shapes in the dark and listened to the rain, its amazing monotonous drumming. He closed his eyes and saw again the softly curved dirty legs of the woman jutting from the tall drenched grass and the Kraut with his dying green eyes, such a dark shade of green, and the red hair matted to the white forehead. That look of pure wonder. Something like a thrill went through him, horrible, and then inexpressible, gone, a feather's touch in his soul, like something reaching for him from the bottom of hell. He looked at the others there with him in the raining dark and was afraid for them, not thinking of himself at all, and it was as if he had already died, and saw them from some other plane of existence.

"*Avete da mangiare?*" the old man murmured. "Eat? Food."

Marson opened a tin of C rations and handed it to him. He ate greedily, with his fingers, as if wanting to get it down before it could be taken away from him.

The others ate, too, in silence. Marson could not do it. He smoked a cigarette and watched them, and then turned his head away. After a time, they were all trying to fall asleep. Marson closed his eyes again and almost immediately fell into a fitful slumber. He saw the old man sneak away into the mist that surrounded them, and then he was trying to stir himself. He heard breathing, voices murmuring, somebody said a name, or cursed, or commanded, and there was motion again and he couldn't break the spell, couldn't make the muscles of his arms or legs move. He was crying out now, in his dream, trying to get them to wake him. *Wake me up!* he was shouting, and then he did stir, into a quiet, a stillness that brought him nearly to his feet, rifle held up, and he looked into the dark, and something moved. But there wasn't any movement and the only sound was the unceasing rain. He looked over and saw that the old man had curled up into his cloak and gone to sleep. The other two were also asleep, Asch with his helmet almost off and his fat cheeks twitching. Asch was probably dreaming of Africa again. "No," he said once, loud. And then again: "No."

EIGHT

Robert Marson had arrived in Palermo on a troopship after the initial fighting there was over. And there had been some delays about further orders. In the area of the war in which he found himself, nobody seemed to know what to do with anybody. Many of them, it was rumored, would be part of an enormous operation somewhere along the coast of France. Others would go to the Italian mainland. They were all training and drilling for amphibious landings. Marson's unit was quartered in a row of pup tents on the outskirts of the city. The Tyrrhenian Sea was visible from their little strip of land. Out in the waters of the harbor there were minesweepers. But it was a peaceful, quiet scene. The idleness made everyone edgy. General Patton didn't want anybody getting too comfortable, or taking it too easy, and so they were performing drills through the early morning hours. But there were delays in deployment, and for a few days they had a kind of vacation. When there was any kind of break, they went into the city and to the beaches nearby and swam in the chilly water and sunned themselves on the sand. They felt an urgency about it all because they knew the war was waiting for them. In the lucid water of the sea, in the brightness and calm of the beach, it was difficult to believe in the war. Marson saw the Palatine Chapel and walked to a Norman castle with several other men.

In a little café off a square, within sight of a mosque, he drank several beers and then two bottles of wine with Saul Asch while Asch talked about his grandfather, the Kaiser's soldier. And about his parents, who were devout, and from whom he had kept the secret of his growing skepticism. "Sometimes," he said, "lies are better than truth. Trust me." Finally he began talking about his wife. A sweet woman. Fifteen years older than he. A teacher who had lived next door all through his growing up. "That's me, buddy. I married the lady next door. A widow, no less. You know how her husband died? Slipped in the bath. No kidding. Fell over and conked his head and that was that. He'd served us iced tea the afternoon it happened. Singing in the shower and the next minute: dead. It doesn't only take war, you know? I knew the guy, too. Nice guy. A little dull. Didn't talk much."

"Asch," Marson said. "You're the most morbid son of a bitch in this army."

"We're all in the crosshairs," Asch said. "That's all I know."

Marson told him about his wife and child. He wanted to try imagining himself to be somewhere after the war, wanted to place himself years away from it in his mind. He carried his wife's letters with him and the little cracked photo of the girl. His wife's name was Helen Louise. The baby's name was Barbara. He had not seen combat yet and he was afraid. He did not want to die or be wounded, of course, but he also feared that he would turn and run when the time came. These others all seemed so certain they would survive, and there were moments in the nights when he believed he would turn and run. He had read the Crane novel about the civil war, and Crane's conclusion—that his fictional soldier had seen the great death and it was, after all, only death—seemed utterly false to him, dangerously, stupidly romantic. He looked at Asch with these thoughts running in his mind and said the names of his wife and daughter, feeling the cold rising at the back of his head, the electric change in the nerves of his spine whenever he received the sense that he would not live to see his daughter or to look upon Helen's face again.

"Nice names," Asch said. "My wife's name is Clara. Sweet lady. When I'm thirty she'll be forty-five."

Marson looked at him.

"You figure?"

"It's more strange if you go the other way. How old was she when you were ten?" He was just talking to keep it all at bay, now.

"Yeah. Jesus," Asch said.

"A little boy."

"When I'm forty-five, she'll be sixty."

"We've got the arithmetic down," Marson said.

"You figure?"

"Fifteen years isn't really so much, is it?"

"Nothing to it, no. Just a thought, you know."

A dark boy came to the table, with a long thin face, beetle brows, a wide mouth, and a leonine shock of black hair. "This wine you're drinking is gutter water," he said, in clear unaccented English.

They were surprised. Marson smiled at him and the boy stared.

"You have a gap in your teeth."

Marson nodded, a little confused.

The boy pulled the skin of his wide mouth back, revealing that he had a missing front tooth. "We're meant to be friends, signore," he said, and introduced himself.

His name was Mario and he was from Messina. He had come to Palermo with his father and brother a year ago, and he knew where all the good wine was hidden. He went on to say that he could speak English so well because he had spent a summer in New York back when he was eight. He had spoken nothing but English that entire summer.

"New York," Asch said, "That's a big city. I'm from Boston."

"I confess I don't like Boston," the boy said. "The Dodgers play there."

"No, that's Brooklyn. Boston is the Red Sox."

"The hated Red Sox."

"My team," said Asch.

"I'm fucked to hear it. I am devoted to the New York Yankees."

"I hate the Yankees," Asch said. "And I hate everybody that likes them."

Mario smiled, showing the wide gap in his teeth. "Then we are sworn enemies, signore." At fifteen, he had yet to begin growing whiskers. He was lean, long limbed, and his hair was so black it showed blue. He told them he had lost his tooth from getting pistol-whipped by a German soldier in Messina. The soldier hit him just for being dark skinned, swiping carelessly across his face with the barrel of the pistol. The boy described this with a smile as if it was all a very stupid joke. The soldier had been shot the next morning from the air by a strafing American plane that had a long-fanged mouth painted on the fuselage. Plenty of teeth in that mouth. Ten soldiers had died in the square from the one pass the plane made, and everybody was sure now that the Germans were through. "I will get you some good wine," he said. "The best wine. Primitivo."

"We'll pay for it," said Marson.

The boy went away and in less than an hour he returned with two bottles under his shirt. The wine was very dark and strong tasting, with a heavy aroma, and the flavor of it lingered on the tongue. It made Marson realize how bad the wine was that they had been drinking.

They were drunk coming back to the unit, and they slipped into their tents as if this were reconnaissance.

The fact was that the whole army seemed confused and not to know where its own soldiers were. There were also soldiers from the other armies—British and Canadian and free French—and there were many combinations of rank, including warrant officers and merchant seamen. Marson and Asch spent time with some of these others, talking about going home and about how maybe the war would end before they had to go where it was. On two other occasions they returned to the café, and each time Mario brought them the good wine.

Other soldiers went into the city and got into trouble. One soldier, a gunnery sergeant, stabbed a man over an Italian girl in one of the saloons. Several people witnessed it and they chased him down and beat him bloody like a dog in the street. The army was going to try him for attempted murder, but then lessened the charge to assault with a deadly weapon. Mario had all of the details.

There wasn't anything to do but unload the ships that kept coming into the harbor. The ships kept unloading troops, too, so the numbers kept getting bigger. There were times when the beaches were crowded, looking like the vacation beaches of home, except that there were very few women. But then the weather turned miserably hot, and several men contracted sandfly fever and malaria. Orders came, forbidding entry into the city anymore.

In the early mornings, in the increasing heat, they went through training and drilling. The first hot days of August were spent in discomfort and sweat work, followed by hours of enforced idleness.

Corporal Marson, halfway up the mountain in the freezing rain near Cassino, remembered how hot it had been in Palermo, and how much he had hated it.

They all hated the inactivity and the waiting and the living out of a pack, not to mention the first and most discouraging matter, being away from home. Home. The word had a resonance that could choke you, and Marson lay awake at night trying very hard not to allow it into his thoughts at all. The thinking itself was terrible. You always ended with the same ache. The idea of never seeing home again burned deep, and he would lie on his side with his knees up and try to pray. Rumors went through the ranks like infection—talk that the Italians would seek an armistice, and that this might truly mean the end of the war. Maybe this would be all there was that they would have to go through . . .

The bells rang from the church spires on Sunday, and the townspeople spoke proudly about how they seemed to sound brighter, clearer, than they ever had during the reign of the Fascists; and all the shops were open. People went back and forth on bicycles and in little cars. Children played in the rubble and dust and in the ponds of water that formed from the few squalls of rain that came in off the sea. It was a coastal city and already there was work on the damages of the invasion.

And the invading force, Marson's portion of it anyway, was stationary, nothing to do but clean and drill and wait. Mario took to coming into the bivouac to see Marson. Merchants, clergy, others were allowed past the perimeter as well. Mario would come in with bottles of wine under his shirt. "For my friend with the hole in his smile," he said.

NINE

O N T H E S I D E of the mountain in the rain, Marson and Asch were awake. Marson decided to let this pause go on a little, for the trembling in his own legs, and the stabbing that he felt with every step. Joyner slept on, though he fidgeted some, his legs jerking. Now and then little plaintive sounds came from him. The old man lay as still as any corpse, cloak pulled half over his head. Marson had also given him his blanket roll. The rock shelter smelled like a basement. There was also the redolence of rotting leaves, mixed with the stale damp odors of the men.

"I don't wanna sleep," Asch said, low. "Ever again. Every time now I go to the fucking desert and see that burning tank. Christ. You figure."

"You've got *me* seeing it," Marson said.

"I don't think I'm afraid of dying. I'm afraid of suffering."

Marson said nothing.

"That woman just stopped. Like that. Dead before she hit the ground. Out like a light. It's worse than the tank, and I'm scared I'll start dreaming that."

"Asch, can we talk about something else?"

"Sure. You wanna plan next year's prom?"

Marson let this go. He shivered and felt once more as if he would retch.

"You believe in God?" Asch said.

"Yes."

"I think it's all one thing. I mean one reason for all of it— the religion and the philosophy and all of the rest."

"Do you mean that all religions are true?"

"They're all there for the same true reason, yeah. It's all trying to explain the one thing. Why we have to die. It's all a puny attempt to deal with that fact."

"Well," Marson said. "That's how *you* see it."

"Listen to the prayers—they're all about save us from it, from the big bad dark. Every single religion. I think they all exist not necessarily because there's a God but because there's death. They're all trying to explain that away somehow."

"Every human civilization or social group, every tribe, believes in a God."

"Yeah?"

"I guess we need a God."

"That's it, then? And you're religious. It's just a practical decision?"

"Yeah," Marson said. And then nodded. "Yeah, sure, why not? Practical."

"Shit, just because you *need* it?"

"But look where that leads. Name one thing human beings need that doesn't exist. We need food, there's food. We need air, air. We need love, there's love. We need hope, there's hope."

"Okay, what about money?"

"You're gonna tell me there's no such thing as money?"

Asch pondered this.

"And there's also how you live your life," Marson told him. "What you do while you're here."

"You mean like shooting a helpless woman in cold blood?"

Marson was silent.

"Yeah," Asch said. "And all this—all this—this destruction—that's a response to it, too. And it's just gonna go on forever or until they find some way to kill everybody."

"Like I've been saying, Asch—you are the most morbid son of a bitch I know."

"'The truth will set you free.'"

"I don't want to talk about this," Marson said. "You think all this hasn't occurred to me? You think I haven't had these thoughts exactly? I don't want to talk about it or think it or hear it said, either. It doesn't do anybody any good. Not now. Not in this mess."

"Fuck," Asch said. "I'm just—talking."

"I agree with you about that—that business back down the road, too," said Marson after another pause. "But we've gotta get through this night, too. Right? What good does it do to argue with Joyner about it?"

"I don't know. He's so sure everything's a joke on everybody else."

Marson drank from his canteen and then held it out to catch the rain.

"I got enough bad imagery in my head to last two lifetimes," Asch said. "I don't know how I'm gonna get rid of it all."

In his mind, Marson saw the eyes of the man he had shot, the curved smudged calves of the woman's legs jutting from the wet grass.

"I don't think any damn church is gonna help me," Asch said. "I wish like hell it could. I'd be in the front row."

"Act as if you have faith, and faith will be granted."

"Is that so. You believe that."

Marson remembered being at a mass in Palermo. The company chaplain, a balding priest named Prentice, said the words *Hoc est enim corpus meum* and held the host up, and Marson believed he could feel the strength flowing into him from the words and what they signified. The church was a bombed-out building, some sort of community hall, and when the mass was over two soldiers walked in casually, talking about the cold water of the beach, and with the practiced gestures of old habit removed the crucifix and the tabernacle, wheeling them aside like so much furniture. Marson, who had remained behind to pray, saw this and was appalled. For a long time the fact of it disturbed him and broke through the flow of his thinking. It gave him a disagreeable sense of being privy to a sordid secret. All his young life, he had been adept

oncentrating his attention, diverting himself from unwanted thoughts.

"My grandfather," Asch said. "The one who fought for the
Kaiser. He was in the war to end all wars, I believe they, uh,
called it. Yeah—that was it. Well, I've read the histories and
the philosophies, too. This is not ideas we're fighting about,
here. No matter what anybody says. They don't like Jews at
home either. Or the blacks. The Nazis' *ideas* don't really mean
shit. It's all just—better weapons. The ideas are just excuses.
Just—we're getting better and better at killing. That's what it
is. We've got the mechanisms for wider and more efficient
killing. It's got nothing to do with ideas."

"You don't really believe that," Marson said.

"If it wasn't the Krauts it'd be somebody else. And it ain't
ever gonna end, either. Not until there's nobody left to kill.
Between 1600 and 1865 you know how many years of collec-
tive peace there were? Years where nobody was killing anybody in armies anywhere in the world? Eleven. Eleven little
years, bud. Think of it."

"Where'd you get that statistic. You made that up."

"I made a study. It's true. And try counting up the years of
peace since then." Asch stared out at the raining dark.

"Christ," Marson said. He saw in his mind the dead
woman's legs jutting out of the drenched grass.

"I guess we have to go to battalion headquarters first," Asch
said. "Don't we?"

"There's the chain of command."

"You wanna talk to *Glick* about it?"

"I guess we go to the captain. An officer anyway. Some officer."

A little later, Asch said, "You think it'll ever stop raining?"

"No."

"I wish we were back in Palermo."

"I wish I was back in Washington, D.C."

"You think Glick would shoot somebody to keep'm from reporting him?"

"Hey—I said I wish I was back in Washington, D.C.," Marson told him. "Try and get some sleep, why don't you."

"Can't sleep. I close my eyes and drift and it's carnival time with the burning tank." Scrunching down against the base of the rock, Asch looked like a puffy little boy in clothes that were too big for him.

They were quiet for a few minutes, and now Marson saw that the other man had indeed drifted off.

TEN

THE GAP IN the corporal's teeth had been caused by getting hit with a baseball when he was about fifteen years old—Mario's age. The ball knocked the one tooth out, and the others grew toward the space, nearly closing it. He explained this to Mario, who wanted to talk about baseball from then on, being, as he said, a New York Yankees fan. No one in the world loved the Yankees like Mario, according to Mario, but among players he had a special affection for the New York Giants player Mel Ott, who lifted his leg when he swung at the ball and still hit home runs. "I know he has failed to hit as many home runs as Ruth, that is true, but Ruth don't have the difficulty of having to lift his leg when he swings at the ball. Is this not right?"

"That's right," Marson said, amused. "You know more about this than a lot of Americans."

"I am a fan. I know from the dictionaries that the first three letters from the word *fanatic* are *fan*."

Marson laughed. "Hell, kid, *I* didn't realize that one."

The boy stuck his chest out. "I love all things from your country."

"Well, I'm impressed. All this from one summer."

"I have followed it in the papers, signore."

"I see that."

Mario shrugged and half smiled, with his missing tooth. "Anyway, I never saw Ruth."

"He was gone by the time you got there."

"Oh, far gone, *sì*. The Chicago team."

"That's right."

"But of his former self, *una voce*. A rumor, yes?"

Marson smiled. "Yes."

"Still, people told me stories about this man so big in everything he did, this *personaggio leggendario,* a fable already."

"A man with a big potbelly from excess," Marson said, making a phantom circle around his middle with his arms.

"Excess," said Mario. "Fat?"

Marson explained about too much of everything.

"Oh," the boy said. "Like my gap-toothed friend and his friend Asch."

Marson grinned. "All right. Sure. Though not as much."

"Little bit," Mario said. "Not as much. Yes."

"Yes. And he—Ruth—he had these spindly little legs, and he could drink twenty bottles of beer and down sixteen hot dogs and still go to the ballpark and hit three home runs in a single game."

"And he also built the ballpark."

"Figuratively," Marson said.

"What is that: *figuratively*?"

"Like a picture. Making a point. He didn't actually build the stadium."

Mario thought a moment. The look of concentration on his face made him wholly beautiful. Marson felt a thrill of affection for him. He had a moment of hoping that if he lived to have sons, all of them would be as inquisitive and expressive and sharp as this dark charming boy, with his habit of reading the English news and listening to radio not to lose the language he had learned in one happy summer in New York.

"I only got to watch Gehrig, and the other one, DiMaggio," Mario said.

The corporal reached over and patted his shoulder. "You're a good man, Mario."

The boy was evidently thinking about having seen the great Gehrig and DiMaggio. "Wondrous players but, you know, also right-handed."

"Well," said Marson. "Gehrig was left-handed."

"He was?"

"I'm sure of it."

"You say Gehrig *was*. He died, then?"

Marson nodded.

The boy frowned darkly, processing the information. He rubbed his lips with the long fingers of his left hand, then held them up and looked at them, as if searching for some answer there, something in the lines of his own palm. "I believe I read that." He sighed. Then: "Yes, I believe I did."

"A great ballplayer," Marson said, wanting to change the subject.

"Well, Gehrig and Ruth and Ott, all left-handers, then. *Sì?* And I am left-handed, too. I love left-handed people and I feel myself to be a brother to them all."

Marson did not tell the other, as he was sorely tempted to do—in that friendly rivalry between boys—that he had been a left-handed pitcher in the Washington Senators organization for almost two years. To do so would've meant having to talk about it, and he did not want to do that anymore, did not want to think about being home and playing baseball, since it dejected him so much and made him realize with such sorrow where he actually was.

Each morning he prayed for the strength to do what would be required, and every single minute he felt like curling up and crying. He kept all this deep inside and never showed any of it to anyone.

Time passed more slowly than he would ever have believed possible. He took to trying to trick his mind by not looking at the time, would do whatever there was to do, forgetting his watch, believing that not to be aware of it could make the passage of the hours seem quicker. He was doing this, working at it one morning, sweeping refuse from the long platform where a temporary mess had been set up. He had seen that it was five minutes past seven in the morning, and he kept his eyes averted, working on, losing himself in the rote motion, imagining what everyone was doing in the late night of back home, the nightclub hour, the hour of all the talk and the music, when the pretty photographers came around and snapped the photos of everyone and offered the pictures for sale, and the cigarette girls walked up and down with their little strapped-on trays and all the choices; it was the hour when people were getting out of movie houses and yawning in the street, waiting for a taxi to take them to some quiet place for coffee or a cocktail. Five minutes past seven o'clock in the morning in Sicily, and Marson imagined it all, back home, a reverie he had fallen into, and when he realized it and shut it off, he felt certain that at least the hour of his dreaming must have gone by. He checked the time again: nine minutes past seven.

Four minutes.

He almost howled from the frustrated rage that came over him. He took the watch off and threw it over the wooden fence that bordered the makeshift mess hall where he was. But then he went looking for it that afternoon with the feeling of trying to find a precious part of life and with the fear of having lost it forever. When he found it, he stood holding it in the shadow of a blasted tree and wept, not even looking around himself to be sure he was alone. He packed it away among his things. And a little later he sent it home, with a note asking his brother to keep it for him.

The gap between his teeth gave him a tough, determined look, whereas Mario, with his missing tooth, just looked simpleminded. But Mario was nothing of the kind. He was quite proud about the wine and claimed that he knew every hiding place the Italians had used to keep the best of it from the Germans. Mario said the Italians—the Sicilians, anyway—hated the Germans more than the Americans or Brits, as he called the English, ever could. The Germans were not slow, he said, but their beliefs made them stupid. Because they believed as they did, they were prevented from receiving certain insights and perceptions, such as the truth that the people of an ancient town like Palermo would have the courage and the intelligence to hide the good wine. It was happening all over Italy, Mario said with pride. The Germans had been fooled into thinking that Italian wine generally was grossly overrated. But Mario would provide Robert Marson (he pronounced it "Mar-sone") with the good stuff.

They were all awaiting orders. The rumors kept flying that the Germans were on the run, and nobody was supposed to talk about any of it. There was a report that General Patton had heard two troops speculating about what Italian coastal city would be the site of the invasion and that he'd had them arrested and sought to have them both shot for treason. General Eisenhower, the story went, had prevented it. Patton got reassigned north, and that fed the rumor that it was true.

All you could do when it came to talk, then, was talk about home. Because home, really, meant everything else, everything that wasn't the war: women, buddies, sports, jokes, music, children, food, drinks, cars, parents, school, houses. Home. But it hurt to talk about home. Marson dreamed of Helen. He put his hands on either side of her lovely face and kissed her, crying. And woke, crying. He wiped his eyes in the dark, buried his face in the pillow, and suffered in hiding.

The weather cooled slightly toward the middle of August and the sky was clear and blue over the darker blue sea in the mornings. The days dragged on. It got easier and easier to believe that nothing would change.

In the evenings, Mario would come around, and Robert Marson would call to him. "Paisan," he would say. "Come play poker with us."

"*Sì*," Mario would answer. "You will all lose money." It was like a ritual speech. They expected the exchange, and they never seemed to notice that it was the same, every time. Mario had told them that he had been taught to play by his father long before the summer he spent in New York. His father had learned the game from the Europeans who used to visit the island before Mussolini and the war and the Germans, back when this, like much of Italy, was a place for wealthy people to come and spend money. "You will owe me your houses," Mario would say, cheerfully. "You will all pay." For Marson, it brought to mind something he had read once, how Caesar had played some card game with his captors, the Gauls, saying repeatedly and jovially how he would escape and come back and hang them all, and how he had indeed escaped and then come back—and kept his word. And Caesar had been an Italian. And the killing had been going on unabated all the centuries. Marson had the thought and considered its uselessness. He did not finally care about any of it, but looked down at his own hands holding cards and wanted them never to be dead, wanted everything in the world to be different and better.

Mario was a bad, inattentive, helplessly social poker player, who wanted to chatter and tell stories and hear stories and seemed not to care a whit about the money, and often he quickly lost what little he had—no one knew where he got it to begin with—and Marson would stake him, for the wine.

"Mario," Marson would say after the first few hands. "Vino."

"Chianti, Mar-sone?"

"Montepulciano, this time."

"Serious."

That was the boy's word, and Marson knew how he meant it, without having to think about it. It was something only between the two of them, a form of respect. A man was serious who asked for good wine and who knew how to appreciate it.

Marson had knowledge about wine because his father had taught him. The old man, Charles, also brewed his own beer, and in the summer of 1929, when Marson was twelve, the workmen building houses in Piqua, Ohio, where the family then lived, would come to the door of the house and say to his mother, "Mrs. Marson, do you think we could have a little of Charles's cold home brew?" Everyone in that town knew Charles, because of the brew and because of what he knew about wine. The German whites, the French clarets, and burgundy. But the old man loved Italian and Spanish wine best. Chianti, and Grenache. And cold, cold beer. When Marson turned fifteen, his father gave him a frosted glass of lager. "You can have a whole life of pleasure with this stuff if you learn to *taste* it rather than look for any strength or comfort in it."

At twenty-six, the young man was familiar with all the available pleasures of good drinking. "Mario," he would say. "Vino. Valpolicella this time."

"Serious," Mario would say.

Marson and Asch would follow him to the edge of the perimeter and watch him go on up the long prospect of the shadowed narrow alley, leading away from the water. The boy would dissolve in distance, and the dark, and they would go back to playing, the game lighted by a candle stuck down into a Chianti bottle, and in a little while Mario would return with the wine, three or four of the unlabeled bottles. It tasted always cool and dry, and they drank it from water glasses and jars, sitting in the flickering light and getting easy in the blood. Marson would lie down on his pallet those nights and, against all efforts not to, would think of Helen, seeing the little half-moon scar—the result of a fall when she was five—below the right side of her mouth, that widened when she smiled.

ELEVEN

CORPORAL MARSON, the only one awake in the freez-ing darkness, considered that he would keep a watch over the others. Maybe the rain would lessen at last, and they could proceed without being drenched. Alone, he opened a tin of rations and tried to eat. His stomach wouldn't accept it. He moved off a few paces, into the downpour, and retched up what little he had swallowed.

He told himself that things had happened too fast for him to think. He replayed the scene in his mind—the shapes in the muddy straw, as if the two people were made out of it, emerging from it in a stream of epithets, the shots from the black Luger, Hopewell and Walberg falling, and his own shot, knocking the man over, the pale German with his bright red hair and his green eyes. It was all out of the realm of time in some way, and then time slowed while the Kraut died, and the woman kept shrieking, and Marson could not take his gaze away from the look of wonder in the dying man's eyes, until he heard the last shot, and turned to see the woman fall over, the legs coming up in that clownish inertia and thwacking back down in the mud. He should have walked over and challenged Glick about it then. The truth was that he had stood staring in sick amazement. He was still filled with that same feeling.

He saw Walberg and Hopewell as they had been that morning and in the hours of the day. He couldn't help himself. He saw Hopewell talking about Miami. The warm air coming in off the sea; the sweet nights with the sound of the waves. "Man, just try if you can and think about the music of the shoreline," he said, "those waves have been coming in like that for millions of years. Makes you feel small. Makes you see how little you are, how insignificant your problems are. Try if you can to think about that water, rolling in under the stars and under the sun over and over like that forever."

McCaig had said, "Try if you can to see how full of shit you are, Hopewell."

"It's true, though," said Hopewell. "I'm full of shit, all right, but that don't stop it all from being true. It's true."

And Walberg, talking about his father. "My dad," he would begin. It was always a story involving the man's prowess. His wit. His escapades, some of which were rather unconvincingly exaggerated. "My dad set a blanket down and put food out for his first sophomore class, a picnic, you know, in the middle of the Lincoln Memorial. Right under Lincoln's statue." A look would come to his dark eyes, an anxious widening of them, as if he understood quite well that no one would believe him, and yet he was compelled to tell the story. Probably it was a story his father told. And it was clear that, for reasons of love, or pride, *he* believed it. Walberg. That boy, with his clumsy ways and his big feet and his soft chin that made him look always as if he were about to cry. Walberg never knew what hit him, and everything of him was gone now, all of it, the memory and the stories and the hope of being as funny and entertaining as the others—the desire to be a storyteller, like Marson—and the generations, too. Generations. His children, and their children. The thought went through Marson like an evil vapor.

Twenty-two years old. Walberg. His parents were probably not yet aware of what had happened to their just-grown boy. Hopewell's parents, too, were probably, like so many, oblivious to what was heading toward them across the awful curve of the world. Hopewell was only twenty. At that age, Marson was pitching a baseball in Charlotte, North Carolina.

He went back to the lee of the rock and nudged Asch awake.

"Christ, not yet," Asch said.

"Tell me," Marson demanded, "why you haven't reported it about the woman."

"I don't know. Leave me alone, let me rest."

"When I was twelve, I saw two guys in a fight. It was the first time I saw anything like it. The sound it made—fists hitting the faces. These two guys, teenagers. They danced and boxed, one coming forward and one backing away, and there was a thin line of blood around the one's mouth—the one who was coming on. They must've traveled a mile or more in that dance. And I followed them."

"Good for you," Asch said. "What the fuck are you telling me?"

"I was fascinated."

"Yeah?"

After another space, Asch said, "You're saying we were fascinated?"

"No. I don't know. I just thought of it—hell."

"I'll tell you," Asch said. "I couldn't believe it and then I could believe it. And it was *not* anything to do with politics or the liberation of Europe, you know?"

Joyner stirred and sat up. "Can you guys shut the fuck up?"

"We should move soon," Marson said.

But then they were all three very still, listening. Something was moving in the trees beyond the ledge. They got closer to the rock, waiting, trying to hear through the sound of the rain. Angelo sat up suddenly, and the sound beyond them stopped. They were all looking out into the pouring dark, and the old man wrung his bony hands and murmured something that sounded like praying. Perhaps five full minutes passed, in which no one moved or looked to one side or the other. The sound was there again, embedded in the incessant thrumming of the rain.

In the next moment, with a kind of haughty obliviousness, a deer walked slowly past where they were. It was a doe, and she stopped to look at them, only half curious, then went on, stepping neatly through the leaf and pine-needle slickness of the way down.

"She better not go down to the road. She'll be breakfast," Asch said.

They were all quiet again, a kind of aftershock from the alarm of something other than themselves moving in the dark. Marson offered Angelo some water from his canteen, and Angelo produced a little bottle of something that smelled of peppermint—it was schnapps. He drank from it and held the bottle toward Marson.

"*Per calore*. Hot your blood."

Marson took a sip. It burned all the way down and caused his gorge to rise yet again. Asch had gone back to dozing, and Joyner, too, seemed to be nodding off. But Joyner had seen the schnapps, and though he was a teetotaler he reached over for it.

Marson said, "This is schnapps, Joyner."

"I don't care. I'm fuck'n freezing." He took a pull of it. "Goddamn," he said, swallowing. "It tastes like candy." When he handed the bottle back, he said, "In a situation like what happened yesterday, everybody ought to keep his fuck'n mouth shut."

Marson made another try with the schnapps, and this time it went down smoothly. He gave the bottle back to Angelo, who put it under his cloak and then sat there nodding and muttering, hands tight on his knees.

"No matter what," Joyner said. "We're all guilty now because we didn't report it. We gotta just keep the fuck out of it."

The rain kept coming. Marson thought of home and then tried not to. He had never seen weather this extreme go on for this long.

Asch sat up and looked around. He had apparently been dreaming again. "Goddamn it," he said through gritted teeth. The old man offered the bottle of schnapps to him and he took it, drank from it, then wiped his mouth and said, low, to Marson, "Where's Mario when we need him."

Marson got up and moved off again, and urinated into the cold running of the rain down the side of the mountain. Here was this humble need, that he had been answering his whole life, and standing there he felt as though he were something set down in the world from a profound distance, another species altogether.

TWELVE

HE HAD MET HELEN when he was eighteen years old. They dated for six years before they were married, and during these nineteen months in the army, he had thought with regret about how he could have been a husband and father much sooner. In that other life he had used baseball as an excuse, a reason not to take on responsibility. He knew that now. He had always assumed he would one day have a family; he believed in that. He wanted to be in the world as his father was. But all of it was something he had imagined in a distance. He was in possession of a talent for throwing a baseball very fast. The ball jumped, moved when he threw it. He was very difficult to hit. And he did well on the farm team. There was talk of sending him up. It became easy to believe he would actually walk out on the perfect green expanse of a major-league ball field and pitch a game. He was that good. And perhaps nothing else would have made his father more proud.

But in the third year, a stubborn tendonitis developed in his throwing arm, and then Pearl Harbor happened, and the war was upon him.

His father had worked for the navy yard since '37, having brought the family to Washington after the failure of the farm equipment business in Ohio. He got the job thanks to Roosevelt's New Deal, and he was a Roosevelt Democrat. This was not an automatic thing with him: Charles Marson knew politics and kept up with all of it like some men follow sports. His own parents had come to America from Frankfurt, Germany, in 1893. He was Lutheran by birth, and he had made a pledge to a dying aunt, who knew of his interest in a young Irish Catholic girl named Marguerite, that he would never convert to Catholicism. He married Marguerite in 1916, with the promise that the children would be raised Catholic. He would not himself go to the church, but he would see that they did. Robert Marson's mother was from Irish immigrants, the Delanceys, all of whom had settled in the Ohio Valley in the middle of the nineteenth century. They had come for freedom—not from political or religious oppression but from hunger. Marguerite had the rare quality of being very devout while also being quite forbearing. She allowed differences between people, and when the workmen in the neighborhood asked for a bottle or two of her husband's home brew, she invariably provided it for them, like a woman in wartime feeding hungry soldiers—all of this while having never tasted any kind of alcoholic beverage in her life. And all of this before the Depression, and the war.

Her husband was tall, strong, blond, fierce eyed, direct, a man whose respect you wanted, and people usually did what he asked them to do. He had a way of talking in pronouncements at times. It was difficult for his children to believe he was not certain of the truth of every utterance. Marson knew his father's self-assurance had a cost: being the oldest, he had been privy to some of the doubts and worries, the hesitations, about the move to Washington. Charles had fought in the first war, in France. He had a shrapnel scar just below his elbow— a lozenge shape of lighter flesh—and on his left wrist and right cheekbone there were beaded lines where fragments of metal had grazed him. He was intensely patriotic, and sometimes his son felt this as an unexpressed—even unaware— form of compensation for the fact that he was of German blood.

Marson's last evening as a civilian was spent at his parents' home, where he and Helen had been living since the marriage. They all had a sad, quiet dinner, Robert, his brother Jack, who could not go to the war because he had asthma, Robert's young sister Mary, Helen, and his parents. Several times the dinner was interrupted by Marguerite's trips to her bedroom to cry quietly into her pillow—it was her way, had always been her habit when something hurt enough to bring tears. Helen sat weeping without trying to hide it, holding the ball of her belly where the baby was, and not eating, but with a cigarette smoldering in the ashtray by her plate. Jack smoked, too, and talked of how he wished he could come with Robert. He wanted to serve. Near the end of the meal, he got up from the table and went up to his room and was gone awhile, and Marson thought he, too, might be crying into his pillow. But he came back down, and he had with him the title of the car Marson had bought in the summer, a Ford sedan.

"What's this?" Marson said to him, only beginning to understand.

"I'll keep it clean as a whistle for you," Jack said. "And of course no one will drive it anywhere until you get back."

"What'd you do?"

"He paid it off," Marson's father said. "You own it outright."

Marson stood and embraced his younger brother, and then stepped back and shook his hand. "You didn't have to do that, Jack. But I'm so glad you did."

"I thought you would be," Jack said, as if he were joking, but his eyes welled up. Marson put his arms around him again.

When it was time to go, he hugged Mary and then his mother, and he allowed her to hold his face in her nervous, thin, cool hands, to look into his eyes that last time. Then he stood holding Helen Louise for a little while, with one hand resting on her abdomen, the lightest touch. His father walked with him out to the end of the sidewalk, where a taxi waited to take him to the train station. Jack and the women and the little girl waited on the porch, Marguerite with a stricken look on her face—but she was not crying now, would not cry—and Helen with her hands folded over the baby in her belly, fingers knotted so that the knuckles showed white. She, too, was managing not to cry, now. Mary was gripping the porch rail, smiling at him through her own complicated feelings. She was only eight, and all this leave-taking, and the talk of the war and distant places, was hard for her to understand. Marson waved at them and blew a kiss. It was a warm twilight, and the stars were beginning to show above the tree line behind the house. It came to him that he had taken this scene, this street, these people, for granted, had simply accepted all of it, and them, as his world. He had a thought: *this is the surround.* Just the word, *surround,* in that sentence, seemed freighted with new meaning. It could not be spelled any other way, was not the word *surroundings.* It was a different word. It was his life itself, containing his home, these parked cars, this house, this sky. Twelve thirty-six Kearney Street, Washington, D.C. *The surround.*

It caught his breath.

His father wanted to have a word with him. The others were shapes now in his peripheral vision.

"I have two things to say to you," Charles said, shaking hands with him.

The younger man held the grip, looking directly back into the somber blue eyes, because he knew it was expected of him. They were two men, standing face-to-face. It meant everything to Marson to be standing there with his father in that way, grown, with a wife of his own and a baby on the way. It caused a little catch in his throat when he tried to speak, so he cleared his throat and kept silent. His father dropped his hand and then put the end of his right index finger on the son's chest, a light but insistent touch.

"Do your duty," he said, and, surprisingly, *his* voice broke. He took a breath, then stepped back. "And write to your mother."

"Yes, sir," Marson told him.

Charles took him suddenly by the shoulders, but then let go. "Remember."

"I will, sir."

"Don't miss the train."

"No, sir."

The old man's eyes were brimming. He had come from Germany. *His* father never spoke a word of English. Marson looked at the porch, Helen's anguished face, his mother's, Jack's, and Mary's, and he raised his hand to wave, then took one more glance at the street, and his father, and with a kind of wrenching shoved his duffel bag into the backseat of the cab and got in.

"Train station?" the cabbie said.

Marson couldn't talk. Through the blur of tears, he saw the cabbie take one look at him in the rearview mirror. The cabbie leaned slightly toward the passenger window and spoke to the boy's father. "I've got a son heading out tomorrow," he said.

Marson's father held up one hand to acknowledge it. Then he stood close to Marson's window. "Come home in one piece. We'll all be praying."

"I will, too."

The cab pulled away, and Marson watched his father's shape grow smaller in the fading light of the street.

THIRTEEN

O N THE COLD HILLSIDE—or mountain—near Cassino, Corporal Marson let the freezing hour pass, dreaming of home. His life there now seemed a hundred years ago. Or it was worse than that: sometimes, now, in the nights, it felt like something he must have imagined. It no longer carried with it the weight of memory but was marbled with the insubstantial feeling of imagination when the faculty for imagining is sketchy or false. He could not really believe it happened, any of it.

And, here, in the middle of a war, in the stupid prodigality of killing all around him, he had been witness to a murder.

He saw Joyner stir and look up. Joyner emitted a soft whimper and then began trying to move his fingers. Joyner turned to Asch, who made a sound like talk, a word that was indistinguishable. "Shut up, Asch," he said. Then he looked at Marson. "It's not a hill. We can't find out anything climbing this fucker."

Asch sat up and put his hands to his face. "I say we go back. That's my vote."

"Shouldn't we go back?" Joyner said to Angelo, who did not know he had been spoken to. "Hey, Mussolini or whatever the fuck your name is."

At the mention of the name, Angelo turned to him. "*Come?*"

"His name's Angelo," the corporal said. "He's our guide. He knows the paths up this hill. You remember me, I'm the one with the stripes."

"Yeah, well ask him if this is a mountain."

"*Montagna, sì.*"

"*See?*" Joyner said.

"Anytime you want to check out, Joyner—you just let me know."

"But, man," Asch said. "I don't think we were supposed to climb a mountain."

Corporal Marson looked at Angelo and made a gesture of questioning.

"Sì," said the old man. "Speaka the English. *Poco.*"

"Well, praise Jesus and pass the fuck'n ammunition," Joyner said.

"If we don't do anything," Asch said suddenly, "we're as guilty as Glick is."

"No," said Joyner. "She's guilty as who *she* was with and she paid for it, too. Maybe you didn't notice that they *shot* two of us."

"*He* shot. She didn't do anything but yell. And die."

"Both of you shut up," Marson said. "There's nothing we can do about it now."

"Just quit talking about it," said Joyner to Asch. "It's getting on my nerves." He was scratching his arm again. "We were all in shock. Forget it, will you?"

"The longer we wait the worse it's going to be."

"You got a radio?" Marson asked him. "Do you?"

Asch merely stared back at him.

"We're going to complete this mission. Got it?"

The old man had a coughing fit, spat into his hands, and then put his hands down in the snow. It felt very strange having him there, and it was difficult to believe that he did not understand everything in their talk.

"Move out," Marson said. He touched the old man on his shoulder and felt bone. For some reason, it got the nausea roiling in him again. The old man sat up and hugged his own skinny knees in the burlap trousers. A few more moments passed while they packed the blankets and gear, and Marson watched Angelo wrap himself in his canvaslike cloak. He thought of his father and wondered if Angelo had many children or grandchildren, a wife who was alive.

An instant passed in which he saw himself trying to tell them at home about the death of the woman.

He shook his head, as if to dislodge something in his helmet. The old Italian man looked at him with a question in his eyes. But no one spoke. They were all about to leave the rock. But then they stopped, each realizing in the same instant that the world had grown hugely, unnaturally quiet. The stillness was startling and appalling. Looking at the dim shapes of one another in that tight little space, it came to them that the rain had stopped.

Joyner held out one hand, brought it back, but then seemed doubtful and put it out again. "Well goodness fuck'n gracious," he said. "Isn't that the sweetest little mothafuck'n thing. You know what it's fuck'n doing now? It's fuck'n snowing."

This seemed to stop them all. Asch gave forth a sound like a gasp and then took his helmet off and looked down into it, as if searching for some secret he had hidden there. He put it back on and sighed. "I think I've got frostbite already in my feet."

Marson remembered the blister on his right heel. He stood. "Let's go."

They moved off the ledge, away from the shelter of the rock, and began to climb again, the old man leading the way. His motions seemed a little stiff now, a little slower. The snow was covering everything quickly, the ground turning white at their feet, and ahead of them, too. It was gathering thickly on the branches of the trees and on every crease in the ground, softening all the crevices and dips and the little ridges and wrinkles of the earth, covering the dead leaves and the windfall as if to hide them all away in whiteness. Walking was becoming even more difficult. The tracks they made were black, and when they slipped there were swaths cut in the whiteness, like wounds. The flakes were very heavy with moisture, dropping with a kind of silent splash, but the flakes themselves did not melt when they hit. They adhered to the surface and were added to, second by second, an impossibly rapid accumulation, and the ground kept getting steeper. Twice the men had to wait while one or the other of them collected himself after a fall—first it was Asch again, and then Marson, who felt in the first loss of footing, as he started down, that he would tumble all the way to the road below. But he caught himself at last, and climbed back toward the others. Joyner gave him the butt end of his carbine and helped pull him up. The old man watched them from the shadow of the floppy canvas hood. He was a dark shape in the whiteness. They all looked like shadows.

Marson's foot had grown progressively even more painful, the pain traveling from his heel to the side of the foot, and now he was experiencing shooting pains all the way to his hip. He called for another pause, and they gathered, a dark knot of shades, amid the black trunks and the outcroppings of rock, huddling together against the cold. They looked around them.

"I think we should go back," Joyner said suddenly, scratching his arm again.

No one answered him.

Marson waved the old man on. And they began climbing once more.

"This is shit," Joyner said. His voice carried in the silence of the snowfall.

Marson ignored him.

They went on without speaking, and their huffing and breathing seemed to grow louder. The snow gathered so quickly, thickening, and now they had to lift their feet out of it and put them back down again, climbing, and the resistance of the gathered snow became another impediment.

Finally they reached another place where the slope leveled

slightly, the brow of a crest, like a landing on a staircase, and this led into a clearing. The trees opened out and fanned to the left and right. The four men walked a little ways into the opening. It was a meadow. They could see the sky here, or something of the sky, a screen of the snowfall with the suggestion of moonlight behind it. Marson reflected that it was light, a kind of light. The snowfield was such a change from the trees, the crowded feeling of the trunks surrounding them as they climbed. They spread out and moved slowly into the clearing. The snow was pristine. There were no tracks and no hollows in it, no sign that anyone had walked here. They stopped again about fifty yards in. The old man fell on a hidden stone, startling the others, and they watched as he quickly tried to rise. The corporal helped him and felt the shivering in his frame. The old man was soaked, and the snow covered his head and shoulders. Marson unfurled his blanket and put it over him.

"It's a fucking blizzard," Joyner said. "We're lost."

"I'll tell you when we're lost," Marson said. But he did not believe himself.

"We could've wandered anywhere in this shit," Joyner told him. "We could be three miles back down the fuck'n road and you know it."

"Three miles *above* the road, I know that," Asch said. He sat down—he seemed partially to collapse—in the snow.

"How much farther?" Marson asked the old man, who stood there shivering, holding the blanket tight around himself.

"*Capisco. Non lontano.* No far. *Ora è vicino.* Near. Near."

"The son of a bitch is lying," Joyner said, scratching.

Asch had lain back on his pack in the snow. "Shut up, Joyner," he said.

"Quiet," said Marson. "We'll take a break here, and then we'll go on."

"We're just gonna stay here until the fuck'n snow covers us."

No one said anything for a moment. And then they were down, facing out from one another, trying to peer into the trees. A sound had come from somewhere, a snapping of something, a branch falling, heavy with the snow—or a footfall. It made them all realize how exposed they were.

"Move," Corporal Marson said, "that way." They headed into the nearest trees, trying to keep low, though this was undoable because the snow impeded every step. They kept having to lift their feet out of it, and it held them, made their flight a strangely farcical lurching and faltering, a ridiculous clownish rush. Asch even laughed, once, high and soprano sounding in the echoless silence, and Marson told him to shut up. The corporal's blistered and inflamed foot stabbed him with each lumbering step. But they all got to the trees and ranged themselves among the trunks, looking out at the blank face of the clearing with their tracks in it, going off in the dark.

After a long interval of waiting and listening, Joyner muttered, "There's nobody else on this fucker but us."

"You want to walk out into that clearing?" Asch said. "You go right ahead."

"I want to turn around and go back down, remember?"

"Well, we can't stay here."

The snow flew at them sideways now, the wind having picked up, blowing across the open space.

"You guys are Christians," Asch said. "You believe in an angry God who's interested in payback. Right? 'Vengeance is mine'—all that. Well, we're gonna pay for yesterday. I think we might be paying for it now."

"You're so full of shit," Joyner said. "Let go of it, will you? It's our religion so we're the ones who'll go to hell, not you."

"I'm not even going to answer *that*," Asch said. "Jesus, Joyner. The way your mind works."

"It's stupid to argue about it *here*," Marson said.

"I can't get the image of her legs out of my head."

Marson almost turned to Asch to say he had the same unwanted picture in his own mind. But the knowledge of it frightened him. He had again the obliterating sense that everything of his memory, everything of his knowledge and his dreams and the hopes and aspirations of his lived life, was in a kind of gray, lifeless suspension. Even the wish to be generous and to seek the good opinion of others. It was all elsewhere.

But he could not think about that now, could not let himself give it room in his mind. There was no place for it there, but only for getting through these hours of the cold and the rising wind.

Joyner and Asch were waiting for him to say something.

He looked out at the snowfield, then at his compass. He

took the scope out of his web belt and panned the field slowly. He could see only the snow inscribing the shape of the wind. "We're gonna go until we can see what's beyond this," he said. "And we're gonna keep to the trees and go around." He took the old man by the elbow. "*Capeesh?* Around? You know the way?"

The old man nodded, gesturing toward the tree line. "*Sì*. Around."

FOURTEEN

They kept as much as possible to the trees, with the dusting of snow limning the trunks on one side, the side where the wind was coming, raising a blinding cloud and stinging their faces. Marson's foot was now burning deep and was strangely numb at the same time. It seemed that the flesh around the abrasion, leading down into the toes, was dead. And the snow made each step a crucible, an agony. He kept trying to offer up the pain, but his concentration was breaking down. The old man's rope-soled shoes were packed with the snow, and he was shaking so visibly that again it became necessary to stop. Marson made the others gather close to him, to try warming him. The corporal's blanket was stiff with freezing, adhering to the old man's frame.

"*Morirò di freddo,*" Angelo said, shivering.

"We don't understand you," Joyner said. "Fucking stupid—"

"Shut up," Marson told him.

"*Morirò.* Die. Wintry!"

"Yeah," said Joyner. "All of us."

"We're gonna have to build a fire," said Marson. "Look for a place away from the field."

"Shit. You think that's safe to do?"

They all waited, facing into the clearing on their left, as if listening for anything like another human presence in the acres of white before them, the crowding trunks behind. There wasn't anything but the sweeping flakes and the wind.

"I don't know," Asch said. "If anybody else is around they're building a fire, too, or they're gonna die."

Once more, they waited.

"Let's just stay awake and alert," Marson said at last, and led them deeper into the trees. They came to a hollow of sorts, a dip in the ground, in the lee of another stone outcropping. Asch and Joyner went off to forage for kindling, and the other two dug out a place just under the curve of the rock. It was difficult to tell which way they had gone now, how far from the other side of the mountain. It was even possible that they had retraced some ground, heading back down toward the road. The snow could've hidden their own tracks from them. According to the compass, they had been moving steadily east.

But the most important thing now was getting out of the wind.

Joyner and Asch were two ghost-dark shapes in the falling curtain of flakes, the wide whiteness out of which the snow-lined trunks of the trees rose. Their squabbling carried back, even in the face of the storm. Marson and Angelo sat against each other side by side, in the lee of the rock. The snow had turned to sleet, mixed now with more freezing rain. They huddled under the declivity, just beyond the reach of the worst of it, and watched Joyner and Asch come stumbling back, their arms full of the windfall for which they had had to dig. It took a while to build the fire, but when it was going, they hunched close, feeling the warmth.

It felt like the first warmth of the world.

Marson watched the ashes and embers rise into the snowing sky and felt them as an announcement of their position. But the crackling of the fire and the groaning of the branches above them were the only sounds now. Clods of snow shook loose from the tops of the trees and dropped like rags among the branches.

In the firelight, he looked at Angelo's face. It was full of wrinkles and faintly dishonest looking—there was something about the way he kept glancing away. He had a long nose, and bony cheeks, and deep-socketed eyes that, in the flickering, suggested the skull beneath the flesh. There was a thin downturning of the mouth on either side, a permanent frown. On his forehead were two marks, upside down Vs, like little scars, and you thought of nails until you realized it was the way the wrinkles in his brow gathered, just under what would've been the hairline. When he opened his mouth to speak, you could see that the front teeth, upper and lower, were all he had, and the upper ones were in bad shape.

"Guide?" Marson said to him. "You know where we go? Guide? Still guide?"

The face did not register understanding.

"Shit," said Joyner.

Asch stared out into the dark, listening for movement.

"Angelo," Marson said, trying to remember what little Italian he had learned from Mario, those months ago—it felt like years—in Palermo. "*Perso?* Lost? Are we lost?"

"Near," the old man said, nodding in the direction of the field.

"He doesn't know where he is any more than we do," Joyner said. "He'd've said anything to save himself. He thought we were gonna shoot him. We're fucked."

"I wish you'd can it for good," Asch said.

"Yeah, let's just bury our heads in the snow. Operation Avalanche, remember? And here we are. Buried in the fuck'n snow." Operation Avalanche had been the name for the landing at Salerno.

"Both of you shut up," Marson told them. "Just shut *up*!"

"I say we head back down to the road. While we can still find the road."

"Near," said Angelo.

"Yeah," Joyner said. "Near. Near what?"

"*Non capisco.*"

"Yeah, no *capeesh*."

"I'm ordering you," Corporal Marson said.

They put some more pieces of wood on the fire. The flames rose higher, and the heat grew momentarily more intense. Asch moved into the circle and put his hands close, and Joyner turned his weapon on the field, where the snow had begun to let up. Above them, an opening began in the clouds, a thinning of the curtain. Something of the moonlight shone through.

FIFTEEN

The difficulty between Marson and Joyner had begun in Palermo. Joyner had been too worried about regulations, and he did not like the use of wine. His people had been very concerned with temperance. None of them drank, not even beer. He'd had trouble with stomach ulcers when in high school, and his mother had had them her whole life. He played in the poker games, but he neither smoked nor drank, and Marson did both, as did Asch and the others. Joyner's fund of curses and obscenities seemed inconsistent with such attitudes, but he did not see the irony. The language he used in daily talk was exclusive of his beliefs about behaviors regarding alcohol and tobacco. Mario, attuned to every nuance between the soldiers, realized this and began looking for ways to needle Joyner with the wine. He would offer it to him every time he picked up the bottle to pour more for Marson or Asch or one of the others.

Joyner tried to ignore him, but you could see that it was getting to him.

"Oh, yes. Signor Joyner does not drink," Mario would say, as if he had to remember it all over, each time.

During the landing drills, when they were put together in the landing craft, and Joyner would spill a stream of his obscenities, Marson would repeat Mario's phrase exactly, with exactly Mario's faintly chiding tone.

They were both buck privates then. Raw, fearful, and antagonistic.

Marson's ability to tell stories was a source of aggravation to Joyner, who liked to think he was good at it. It seemed to others that Marson had led a more interesting life, and of course he was older. Marson's time in boot camp included episodes of wild stupidity by a big brutal boy from Texas, named Wagoner, who got drunk every day somehow and deserved everything that his stupidity brought him. Marson had told a story about how Wagoner, after being stripped of his rank because of a fight he had picked at a saloon on the perimeter of the base, came to Marson and asked what he should do about the darker place on his sleeve, where the one stripe used to be. Marson, who had Wagoner's trust because he was a storyteller and because the stories commanded the attention of others, told him to go to the supply shack and get some stencil letters and print DISREGARD on the sleeves. Wagoner had done so and had walked around the camp that way, through most of an afternoon, until a sergeant finally noticed it and chewed him out for not being in uniform.

Marson went on: "The DI would scream at the guy, 'Damn it Wagoner, don't you know we're at war?' And Wagoner would say, 'You know it, Sergeant, and boy I sure hope we win.' He had a sweat of booze on him every single morning and I swear I don't know where he got his hands on it."

"You don't know where I get the wine," Mario said. "But I am never mean or dumb."

"You bring it back, Mario, my friend. This guy drank it all. He never gave anything to anyone except a black eye or a busted lip."

Mario liked the story about the stripe and the stencil so much that he had the word DISREGARD scrawled on the sleeves of his T-shirts, and he was always after Marson to tell more Wagoner stories. Wagoner being carried asleep in his bunk out of a barracks and onto the gravel walkway that ran down the center of the camp. Wagoner getting drunk on Aqua Velva and passing out in the chow line. Wagoner curling up with his blanket roll so he could sleep better while on guard duty during war games. That was what finally got him washed out of the service, unfit for duty.

"Unfit for duty," Joyner said. "Smell that one."

The word *washout* became a favorite expression of Mario's, and he took to calling Joyner that, whenever Joyner would turn down yet another offer of wine.

"More wine, Signor Joyner?"

"I'm not even gonna answer you."

"Ah, a washout, then," Mario would say. Clearly, he was Marson's friend. And when orders came down and they were all gearing up for what they knew would be an amphibious landing somewhere on the mainland, Joyner came to Marson and said, "Your Guinea pal has got something for you."

"Wish I could take it with me," Marson told him. "Call him Guinea again and I'll fix your smile for you permanently."

"You can try to," Joyner said.

They were standing in the middle of the camp, which was being dismantled. They stood very close, and neither of them moved for a few seconds.

"Maybe you should save your anger for the Jerries and the Wops," Joyner said.

"Oh, I'm not angry," said Marson. "I'm just definite."

"Well, let's see how definite you are in ten minutes."

All around them, men were putting things into duffel bags and packs. It was a little frantic. This would be an enormous transporting of men and supplies, and they were going to be in the middle of the war and they knew it. They knew that a lot of them would be dead soon. The pall of that knowledge colored everything and made the sunny breezes from the sea seem dimly wrong even as they also felt unbearably precious.

"Your boy has something for you," Joyner went on, "and I'm not talking about your fuck'n wine." He pointed up the row of tents being dismantled. There was Mario, with a small boy and a man. The man had his arm around Mario's shoulder. All three of them were being prevented from entering the bivouac. Marson walked over to them.

"Signor Mar-sone." Mario smiled brightly with his missing tooth. "This is my father. Giuseppe."

Giuseppe was squarely built, bulky through the shoulders, with muscular arms and big, rough-looking hands. His face was large featured—a wide nose and round, heavy-lidded eyes, and a black hairline that came to the middle of his forehead. He said something to Marson in Italian, glanced at Mario, and then back at Marson. *"Per favore,"* he said.

"I'm sorry," Marson told him. *"Non parlo italiano."*

"This is my father," Mario said. "He's embarrassed by his English, so he speaks Italian to you." He made a motion as if to present the little boy, pushing the boy's skinny shoulders so that he stepped forward. The boy was even darker than Mario, sullen seeming, with a little purple scar the shape of a fishhook above the left eye. "My father wishes you to take my brother with you to America," Mario said.

Marson looked at him, and then at the boy, who was staring at his own small hands folded in front.

"Per favore," said the man. *"Per favore."*

"I—" Marson began.

"I know you can't take two of us. And my brother has never seen America." A light shone in Mario's eyes—a kind of sorrowful humiliation, a regret, and something of pride and anger, too. "You must take him for the wine, Signor Marsone."

"Wait. Lord. Look," Marson said. "You think we're—"

"Il Duce will not last," Mario said. "Italy will surrender. It is over. Will you do it?"

"But I'm not *going* to America." Marson felt anger and tried to suppress it. "I wish I was. Look, Mario, I'm probably going to be dead tomorrow. We're all probably going to be dead. We're not—we're headed to the mainland. The invasion. Tell your father. It's an invasion. We're not going home. We're going to the war."

The man said something else in Italian, then turned to Marson. "*La mia famiglia.* Family."

"I understand," said Marson. "My family's five thousand miles away."

The man stared.

"*Capisco,*" Marson said.

"*Sì. Come voi, amo la mia famiglia.*"

"Like you," Mario translated. "He loves his family." The look in his eyes was almost ferocious.

"I do understand," Marson said. "I wish I could help."

Mario muttered something in the other language to his father, who appeared confused for a moment, but then, quite slowly, showed the resignation of a man used to things turning out badly. With a sorrowful nod of his head he took the little boy by the hand and turned with him.

"I sell the wine," Mario said. "To the others I sell it."

"Yes."

"You, because of the hole in your smile. I get you the best."

"I know. I wish I could do something more." Marson had twenty dollars of overseas scrip in his pocket. He reached in and brought it out, a ten and two fives. He handed Mario the ten and one of the fives.

The boy glared at him, but took it.

"It's all I've got." Marson offered him the other five.

"You are a friend," Mario said. "Serious." And he walked away.

Marson watched him go. There was confusion and noise all around him, planes going over, and men shouting back and forth about the hell they were all headed to. It sounded like a lot of boys excited about going to a football game, until you heard the controlled desperation in it.

Joyner had come partway to the end of the row of tents, and he stood waiting. "You see what your goddamn wine drinking got you," he said.

Later, on the troopship headed for Salerno, news came through on the radio that the Italians were out of the war. Mussolini had been deposed. Everyone celebrated, and Marson had the thought that the mainland might be the same as it had been at Palermo. For some reason this gave him a terrible pang of missing home, of some kind of waste. The feeling surprised and alarmed him, and he looked out at the rise and fall of the sea, its little churning whitecaps, and was amazed at his own mind. Joyner came up to him and said, "We might actually miss this fuck'n war." He smiled and patted Marson on the shoulder, turning to gaze at the sea and sky with him. Asch walked over and offered Marson a cigarette. "Lucky Strike," he said. "Good name for a cigarette."

"That actually smells good," said Joyner. "You guys make me wish I smoked."

"You want one?" Asch said.

"Hell, sure—why not?"

Asch lighted it for him. He drew on it and did not cough.

He kept the smoke in for a long time. When he let go of it the cough came, and the other two pounded his back and helped him through it.

"How do you guys stand it?" Joyner said, still coughing.

"You get used to it," Asch said. "Takes work. I've been practicing to get better at it most of my life." He drew on his own cigarette and blew the smoke. Joyner tried it again and coughed less this time.

"It hurts my pipes, though."

"Maybe you should go easy the first time," Marson told him.

"Naw, I'll finish it."

They watched him smoke. He was getting the hang of it. He looked at Marson. "How much scrip did you give Mario?"

"All I had."

"You're gonna wish you'd kept some of it when we get to the mainland."

"It's only money," Asch said.

"That's kind of an unusual thing—" Joyner stopped. "Yeah, right. It's only money. Fuck it."

Asch shook his head, but smiled. There were cheers going up all over the ship.

They smoked their cigarettes and then tossed the butts over the side. In the happy feeling of the day's news, Marson stood between them and put his arms across their shoulders. Looking out at the red sun going down over the slow, ponderous agitation of the Mediterranean, he forgot all the tensions and slights and irritations of the last few weeks and felt as if these two were, after all, the best friends a man could have.

SIXTEEN

CROUCHED CLOSE TO THE FIRE, in the woods beyond the snowfield, Corporal Marson thought of the futility of money, and then he was thinking of the futility of everything. He tried to pray, and the words went off from him, as if addressed to the wind and the silence all around. Joyner had opened a can of vegetable hash and was heating it in the flames. He wolfed it down, someone filling a little hole, tasting nothing.

The old man watched him and then, seeing Marson's quiet gaze, looked down.

"Food?" Marson said. "*Mangiare?*"

The old man shook his head and smiled thinly. Marson wondered what he might be like, sitting at a table with people around it, and wine, and a peaceful countryside out the windows of a room. A warm countryside. He imagined it, the green grass in the gold light of an evening's sinking sun. And then he moved closer to the fire, shuddering. Joyner had finished with his rations and he tossed the empty can off into the snow, like a grenade, the same motion of the arm.

"I could be a father right now," Asch said suddenly. "That seems like an insane thought to me."

"You better quit thinking so much," Joyner said to him, reaching under the sleeve of his field jacket and digging at his forearm.

Asch ignored him, still looking at Marson. "Can't we call it, and go back down?"

"Asch wants to go back as much as I do," Joyner said.

Marson turned to the old man. "Take us."

"*Non capisco.*"

He gestured toward the clearing. "Near. Bring us near. We move near."

"Oh, *sì.*"

He gathered his cloak about him and stood. The others followed suit. The wind had dropped now, and the last of the snow filtered down out of the opening sky. Corporal Marson saw a glitter in the farthest distance, just above the tree line. The North Star. It thrilled him. There were little places in the sky beyond the trees, where the clouds were parting, like the fingers of a giant hand, once clasped, now letting go.

They covered the smoldering fire with snow and trudged on, keeping to the trees, going around the field, another path the old man knew. He moved with the alacrity he had exhibited in the first hour of the journey. On the far side, the ground dipped for a few yards and then rose sharply again, and again they were climbing. But it was just the cold now, and the snow that had already fallen. They saw no tracks, no signs of life anywhere, until they reached another clearing, a small white level span of ground, leading to another tree line and more of the steep climb. In that clearing, standing quite still, was a large buck deer, with a prodigious rack of antlers ranged above its head. It was looking right at them, white breast jutting from just below the neck, its breath showing in frosty vanishing plumes from its black muzzle. The eyes were black, blank, staring. Marson felt eerily as if it had been sent by the doe they had seen earlier, to evaluate what sort of threat they were to the forest. It turned, so slowly as to seem gradual, then stepped away, thin legs looking almost spindly, the massive tawny-black shape adorned by the high white tail, moving off. It came to a large windfall, the trunk of a fallen tree, and leapt over it with swift ease, as though its containment in gravity were only provisional.

"Jesus Christ," Asch said.

They watched it go up through the trees, in the next level of this mountain they were climbing.

"There's no end," said Joyner, sounding as though he had wept the words out.

They came to the ascending ground and began climbing again, following the old man. There were tree shadows now, and Marson realized that the moon was high, and it had cleared the clouds in the lower quadrant of the sky. A clear night. The air was colder than it had been all day. It stung his bronchial tubes, yet he drew it in, felt the purity of it, the new, dry, clear air.

They were climbing. It was rote again, their thighs burning, the ground treacherous and shifting beneath them. For a time, the men followed the tracks of the deer, going off up the incline, but then the tracks wound through the trunks of the trees and disappeared.

"I've gotta shit," Joyner said suddenly. "God*damn* it."

They stopped. He went a few feet into the moon shade and took care of it, cursing. Angelo made a sound under his breath. There was no telling if it was a word or merely a grunt.

"God*damn* it," Joyner said, off in the near distance. The noise of what he was doing went off from him and carried over the stillness.

Asch made a little snorting sound, a muffled laugh. "He's louder than a tank."

"*Il suo culo congelerà,*" the old man said.

"*Congelerà.* What the hell is that?"

"*Freddo.* Ice. Freeze-uh." The old man made a motion of being cold, arms wrapped around himself.

"Freeze-uh his ass, right?" Asch laughed. "Ass?"

"*Culo. Sì.* Freeze-uh his ass."

"Freeze-uh his *culo,* that's right." He kept laughing.

Joyner took care of himself as best he could with fingers that had grown numb and paper from his pack that was damp and cold. He cursed and sputtered.

They went on a little and then stopped to wait for him. The wind had died down, and there were very few clouds now.

Joyner had finished and commenced getting himself together again, still cursing. From this distance, he sounded like a complaining little boy. He trudged up to them without making eye contact.

"*Siamo arrivati,*" said the old man, gesturing at the steep rise ahead. "*Quello è il posto.* There. Over there."

Joyner cursed again and muttered. Marson didn't hear him, and then he did. "We must be in fuck'n Switzerland by now."

"*La Svizzera,*" the old man said.

"Yeah, you understood that, motherfucker."

They kept climbing. The ground leveled again and they saw that it stretched out away from them; they saw trees that looked short, like a tight row of firs, until they realized that they were the tops of trees. They had reached the crest and started across it, hurrying without realizing it, the old man leading the way.

They had gone about twenty yards when they heard a shot. One report, from no direction they could pinpoint. They all dove into the snow, even the old man.

After a few seconds of waiting, Marson murmured, "Anybody hit?"

Silence.

"Joyner?"

"I'm here. Goddamn it."

"Me, too," said Asch.

The old man murmured. "*Madre di misericordia . . .*"

"That was a shot," Asch said, low. "A pistol."

"Did you get a sense of where?" Marson asked him.

"Shit—over there?" Asch pointed to the trees on the far side of the hill.

"You're sure it was a shot and not a branch breaking."

"It was a shot. Christ."

"But it was far. It was a long way away."

"You sure of that?"

"You can't tell distance at this height," Joyner said.

"Sound carries farther the higher you go, doesn't it?" said Asch.

They were whispering, but the whispering itself carried. It made them all the more nervous about what might be out there on the other side of the hill.

"Keep down," Marson said. "And stay quiet. Get back to the trees."

The wind had picked up again, rising from the north, and it lifted the snow, as if the hill, this meadow, were in the wildest heart of weather, above the snow line. It was the wind of the tops of mountains.

"Climb the hill," Joyner said. "Fuck." His scratching now looked frantic, as though something were crawling on him under the sleeve of the field jacket. "Go right on up the brow of the fuck'n devil."

"One more word like that from you," Corporal Marson said, "and I swear I'll shoot you myself."

"Fuck you, okay? This old man's led us on a wild goose chase."

"Shut *up!*" Asch said. "Marson's in charge."

They were still whispering.

"Close," the old man told them.

"It's all shit. We don't even know what's going on down on the road. The fuck'n Jerries could've turned on them and we're in enemy territory now."

"Shut up," said Marson.

They were quiet again, listening.

"We were fucked the minute Glick shot the whore," Asch said suddenly.

"Oh, that's great, Asch. We're cursed. Christ."

"*Madre di Dio . . .*"

"Everybody shut up," said Marson. "That's an order!"

The wind came over them with more force, and it made a sound, moving through the trees. The high, bare branches clicked and groaned and cracked. They were still heavy with snow and ice.

"How long do we stay here?" Asch said, low.

"Let's go," said Marson. "We'll go around again. Keep to the trees."

For a while they moved with stealth, from tree to tree, pausing a little at each one to listen. There was only the wind.

At last they came to a long narrow swath of open ground, between two rows of trees, with drifts of the snow in it. It was two banks, really, and it looked like a riverbed, or a lane. They went along it, crouching low, toward a large black object, a rock or a hillock, you couldn't tell. It blocked the bed, and when the old man reached it he abruptly stopped and held one hand out, waving them down. They scrabbled into the snow-laden second growth and waited, watching him where he knelt, using it for cover. They could see now that it was the root system of a big fallen tree. They heard water trickling somewhere. The old man waved them forward, and Marson went over to him. Just on the other side of the tree trunk was a small stream. It amazed him that the water was not solid ice. But the ice was melting. Just beyond the melting were the smoldering remains of a fire, and, within a few feet, a dark elongated shape.

In the instant of understanding that the fire was the reason for the melting, Marson realized that he was looking at the body of a man, lying flat on his back, arms outstretched, as if he had fallen backward and been left that way.

SEVENTEEN

IT WAS A GERMAN SOLDIER, from the markings on his uniform, an officer. He had no effects with him, or near him. His helmet was gone. His overcoat was missing. The pockets of his trousers had been turned inside out. In the middle of his forehead was the perfect round blackness of the hole the bullet that killed him had made. The snow under his head was stained, and much of the snow beyond where he had fallen was splattered and dark. It looked black in the moonlight. His eyes were black, too, and open wide.

"Goddamn, I wanna go down," Joyner said, scratching. "This is fucked. This is fucked, man."

"Why would they shoot their own guy?" Asch said.

No one answered. Marson told them to get down, and they did so, because the old man had got down. They waited. None of them could see beyond the slope of the corridor of snow between the rows of trees. The little embers of the fire were still warm. There were many tracks in the snow around it.

"They've left him," Marson said, low. "And they haven't tried to hide that they were here. So either they're running, or they don't know *we're* here."

"*Tedesco,*" said the old man, peering out from the tree roots.

They crouched lower, quickly, and looked out. But the old man was apparently only commenting on the body.

After a few tense moments of watching, Marson said, "Yes. *Tedesco.*"

"What the hell are you saying to him?" Joyner demanded.

"The word means 'German.'"

"Well talk English, for Christ's sake."

They held quite still. There had been another sound. But it was just the wind stirring in the branches again. Snow dropped from one of the treetops, like a collapsing roof, and broke among the lower branches.

"We didn't see any tracks getting here," Marson said.

"We made contact," said Joyner. "We can turn around and go back down this fuck'n thing."

"It's all fucked because of the whore," Asch said, low. He spoke evenly, but in the moonlight his face looked contorted with fright.

"I want you both to shut *up,*" Marson hissed at them.

"*Tedesco,*" said the old man.

Marson turned to Asch. "How many men do you think? From the tracks."

Asch leaned up and looked at everything. "I don't know. Ten?" They were whispering.

"It's more than ten," said Joyner. "If you ask me it's a *lot* more."

"Do you think they knew we were coming?" Marson asked.

"What the fuck are you saying?"

"They don't know about us," Asch said. "Or they don't care about us."

"I don't think they know," said Marson.

After another pause, listening for sounds, he murmured, "We'll wait a little. Let them get a good head start if they're running. And we'll be ready and waiting if they're coming back."

"Jesus Christ," Joyner said. "Aw, Jesus. You think they'll come *back*?"

"Just keep your eyes open," Marson said.

The old man had hunkered down against the tree trunk, with his knees up and his lower face covered by the cloth of his hood. It was so cold, here. From the moon shade, his old eyes seemed ghostly. He stared at Marson. "*Freddo mortale.*"

"Cold," Marson said.

"*Sì. Freddo.*"

"We stay here for a time. *Capeesh?*"

"Stay, *sì.*"

Marson looked through the scope, panning slowly across the open space and along the line of treetops beyond. The trail of footprints led away from the little campsite, and the wind, even now, was covering many of them, blowing the snow like sand. It was stronger and more steady now.

"It blew like this in Africa," Asch said. "But it was sand. I'd rather have the sand."

They fell silent again, waiting and listening. It was hard to say how much time went by. Before them, the body of the dead German was being gradually effaced by the blowing snow. The wind had shifted, coming fast from the west. Marson kept looking at what was left of the dead man's hair, and how the wind disturbed strands of it. There wasn't much that was clearly distinguishable anymore, because the drifting from the wind in its new direction kept sweeping across the little campsite, covering the embers, the tracks, the folds of frozen cloth on the body, and the features of the face. Had they just now stumbled upon him, they would not be able to say what army he came from.

Asch moved back into the trees and urinated. When he returned he came low, gasping. He looked at Marson with a pleading expression on his face. But he said nothing.

"Go ahead," Joyner told him. "Make your complaint. It's cold. You frosted your little dick."

"I'm going to report what happened," Asch said.

"Jesus. *That* again. Mr. Broken Record."

"I'm reporting it. That's all I'm saying. I'm not going to go the rest of my life carrying this."

"Hey, who made you the moral compass of the fuck'n Fifth Army."

"I said we'd talk about it when we get back down to the

road," Marson said. "This isn't the time. I'll go with you when the time comes."

"You're both fucked," Joyner said.

Marson kept glancing at the old man, who appeared simply to be observing the others as a man gazes upon birds feeding and arguing on a shoreline.

"Like I said, you might've noticed that two of us got it when she fell out of that cart."

Asch said, "She didn't do the shooting. For all we know she was a refugee, a victim."

"She was a Nazi, man. They don't like Jews. That's your people, isn't it?"

"Hey, fuck you, Joyner. *You're* a Nazi."

Joyner started toward him, but Marson got between them and held his carbine up, so that the barrel end nearly touched Joyner's chin. "Not one more word, not one more inch— *nothing,* Joyner."

The other's eyes were full of defiance, but he crouched back down and kept digging at the place on his forearm, muttering something about the itch that wouldn't stop.

Marson turned to Asch, still holding the carbine up.

Asch said, "Otherwise, we're no different than *they* are."

"Gotta have the last word," said Joyner. "Take it away, asshole."

"Close," said the old man.

"Sure," Marson said. "Near."

But they remained where they were, looking out at the snow corridor between the trees, the body lying there with the snow drifting over it.

EIGHTEEN

THE WIND GLITTERED WITH SNOW, and the cold moon rose higher. It was sharper and brighter at the height of the sky. Corporal Marson thought of the stars as ice crystals. The trees made complicated striations of shadow, and the effect was like a ghostly daylight. Nothing moved before them. There was no sound anywhere but the wind. Marson watched Joyner where he crouched in the lee of the tree trunk with his carbine across his thighs, scratching the place on his forearm. The corporal believed now that the itch, as much as anything else, defined him.

At Palermo, when he first began to talk about the skin problem, there was no swelling or rash, no marks, no discoloration, just the itch. It had first come up when they were playing poker, and everybody but Joyner was drinking Mario's wine. Joyner would scratch the arm, and then scratch it again. He would look at it and shake his head, and then start once

more, scraping and rubbing, looking at it and frowning. "Goddamn," he would say. And he would look along the arm, trying
to find what it was on the skin that made it itch. He showed it
to the others, and no one could see anything but the places
where he had scored it, digging at it. He showed it once just as
the itch began. The hair of the forearm stood up, as if some
kind of static electricity were at work. "Look at that," Joyner
said. "You guys tell me. That's the only thing it does, and then
the itch. It's driving me out of my fuck'n mind." He grabbed
the arm and scratched. "God*damn* it."

This kept up for days. He thought it might be sand flies, or
chiggers, but the medic found no trace of any poison or bite.
Joyner would keep scratching until it bled. And only after it
bled would the itching stop. But then it would commence
again a little farther up the arm or down toward the wrist,
within an inch of the original site. The medic called it Irish
skin.

"I'm nuts with it," Joyner said. "I want to cut the goddamn
skin away. Peel it the fuck *off.*"

That was way back at Palermo.

Now, he sat hunched over in the cold, huddled in the torn
root system of the downed tree, and dug at himself, muttering
low, glaring out at the moon-bright field, the top of the mountain. They were only a few hundred yards to a falling off, the
descent on the other side. Marson watched him and worried.

"Put some snow on it," Asch said irritably. "Numb it."

"Fuck you."

They watched the field, the open ground. The old man

began to cough. He choked up something and spit it out, then pulled snow over it, looking apologetically at Marson.

"How old do you think he is?" Asch wanted to know.

Marson said, "Angelo—how old?"

"*Non capisco.*"

"*Età.* Your age." He knew the Italian word from Mario.

"Oh, *settantasette anni.*"

Marson turned to Asch. "He's whatever that is."

"Seventy?" Asch said.

"*Sì.*" The old man shrugged.

"More than seventy." Asch gestured, raising one hand over the other.

"*Sì.*" The old man seemed confused.

"Goddamn," Asch said. "More than seventy. You're in some shape, ain't you."

"Good strong," Angelo said. "*Molti bambini.*"

"*Bambini?*"

"*Sì.*" The old man held up both hands, fingers extended. He closed the hands and then opened one of them, extending four.

"That's fourteen," Asch said. "Damn."

"How many grandchildren?" Marson asked.

Angelo stared, smiling, and slowly lifted both hands again, all fingers extended, closed them, and then opened them again, and then closed them, and then held up the one hand with three fingers extended.

"God," Asch said. "Twenty-three?"

"That's too many Catholics," Joyner said. "Too many

mackerel snappers." He laughed at his own joke. "How many of them are still alive."

This occasioned a silence. Marson did not know whether or not Angelo understood the question. His face was difficult to read. He looked at Joyner and seemed to be waiting for him to go on.

"Still alive," Joyner said. "*Capeesh?*"

"*Sì,*" the old man said. "All."

"You're a lucky Fascist."

Angelo shook his head. "No."

"Not lucky?"

"No."

"Do us a favor, Joyner, and shut up," Marson said.

"Where's your family?" Joyner asked. Then he looked at Marson. "Get him to tell you where they are."

"Roma," the old man said.

"You understand more English than you're letting on, huh."

The eyes gave no sign of comprehension.

"He knows," Joyner said. "And I bet he can tell us what's on the other side of this fuck'n mountain we're climbing."

"We know what's on the other side," Asch said. "The fucking war."

"I just don't think we should trust him."

"*La mia famiglia,*" the old man said. "Roma."

Joyner kept digging at himself. "Shit. You guys—just remember this son of a bitch was part of the Axis, okay? And he's seventy—which means he was around for Albania and the Africa stuff, at the beginning. Ethiopia—all that."

"What about Ethiopia?" Marson said. "What the hell are you talking about?"

"It goes back ten years and more," Joyner told him. "These guys've been fighting a long time. I'm sure they're sick of it, but some of them are probably sick in other ways."

The old man understood that they were talking about him. He kept smiling, clearly trying to show good will. Marson felt ashamed and tried to soften the old man's anxiety. He nodded at him and then offered him some water from his canteen. The old man took it, keeping one eye on Joyner.

Joyner said, "You don't fool me, pie-zan. I ain't like these guys."

"*Molti bambini*," Angelo said, smiling and nodding.

"Wouldn't surprise me if you know every word we're saying."

He kept the smile, but glanced away.

The wind suddenly died down once more, and all around them was deep stillness. Beyond the root tangle at the foot of the downed tree, the dead soldier was like another part of the woods. The snow had covered the legs and filled wrinkles in the tunic, and it had gathered at the neck and in the ears. It kept drawing their gaze to it. Nothing stirred anywhere else.

"Shit," Asch said to Joyner. "Think of it as a statue."

"How long do we have to fuck'n stay here," Joyner said, digging at the place on his arm.

"Not much longer," said Marson.

The old man coughed again, and this time it became a fit.

He held his hands over his mouth, attempting to muffle the noise. The coughing went on.

"Great. Let's send up a flare," said Joyner. He grabbed a handful of snow and packed it into his sleeve. "Fuck'n freezing. And I've gotta put ice on my fuck'n arm."

Asch stirred suddenly and scrabbled through the snow a few feet away and was sick there, noisily, with a terrible-sounding loud belch. Then he groaned and was sick again. He came back and crouched with his back against the tree trunk. "I didn't even know I was gonna do that."

"You all right now?" Marson asked him.

"I don't know." He indicated the corpse lying only a few feet away. "I can't stop looking at that. I just got a feeling, like a jolt, like a—like a sudden remembering where I am. And I thought of the whore. It got me. Let's get out of here and get a look over the other side and then get our asses back down to the road. Jesus."

"Near," said the old man.

"If he says that one more time I'm gonna blow him to Sardinia," Joyner said.

"Man," Asch said. "Let up a little."

"I don't wanna die on this fucker."

"Stop talking shit," said Corporal Marson. "We're gonna wait another fifteen minutes. Be quiet and listen and maybe we won't die."

Again, they were silent. The quiet stretched on away from them. It was impossible to believe that there was a war on the other side of the hill, beyond whatever hills there were. But then another little breeze stirred, and it brought a sound to them, a distant hum. Marson thought he might be imagining it. Asch said, "What the hell is that?"

Joyner, holding his arm, said, "Planes."

"No," said Marson. "Tanks."

"Jesus Christ. Up here?"

"No."

"*Carri armati,*" the old man said.

"Near?" said Joyner, spitting.

"No, signore."

"Yeah—we'll find out that 'near' means the fuck'n Jerries."

"It *is* tanks," Marson said. "Come on, move out." He indicated for the old man to lead the way.

They followed him, past the body of the dead German, across the corridor of snow and into the trees, up another swale of ground, and then a path down again, more and more steeply, so that several times they slid in the snow and had to hold on and pause. There were a large number of foot tracks where they walked now, and they kept low, moving once more from tree to tree with stealth. The old man was doing the same. They had been doing this for some time before it came to Marson to wonder whether he himself had started this or had followed the lead of the old man. He was too exhausted to think. He looked at the moon in the starry sky and understood that they had not yet crossed midnight. At a wide, extended stairlike ledge of rock, he signaled the old man with a tap on his back to stop. They all slid out on the first tier of the ledge to look down. There was another snowfield, perhaps fifty yards across, and the crowding tops of more pines. Beyond that was another mountain, other mountains. The snowfield was heavily marked up with foot tracks, all going away.

"They came through here after the snow stopped," said Marson.

"Near," the old man said, nodding.

Marson turned to Asch and Joyner. "That shot we heard— it was what we left back there. Whatever—"

Asch interrupted him. "It took you until now to figure that out?"

Marson went on, more slowly. "Whatever they're up to, it's got nothing to do with us. So let's see if we can get a look at what they're running to, from a distance, and then go back down."

"We gotta go *up* again before we go back down," Joyner said.

Marson said, "We'll give them a little time to get farther away."

They moved back off the ledge and down, to the hollow beneath it. A mound of drifted snow hid them and kept them from the stirrings of the frigid air. Marson's clothes were almost dry now, from the outside in, the wind having taken care of the outer surfaces. His underclothes were still soggy and they clung to him in all the wrong ways. The others were suffering the same discomforts. They ate some more rations, and Asch passed his canteen, then filled it with snow and put it back.

"We're gonna have to climb this fucker again, you know," Joyner said.

Asch said, "We know they're going away, don't we?"

"A little farther," said the corporal. "If we get to where we can see down to the road from a distance, we'll know more."

"How much do you wanna know?" Joyner said. He was scratching his arm again, pulling at the snow and using it to freeze the abraded place.

The wind picked up once more, a cold scarf lashing across their faces.

"I want to know enough. What we were sent to know. And shut up."

"Why'd you pick me for this fucker, anyway."

"I didn't pick you. Glick did."

"Glick's a killer," Asch said. "We're soldiers. He's a killer."

"Listen."

They paused. Far away, barely discernible, the wind was carrying another sound. Shooting. It was shooting. Unmistakable. But not a battle or a skirmish. The shots seemed timed—spaced at nearly exact intervals. Each of the men looked at the others, each trying to solve the problem of the sound and what it meant. It occurred to them almost simultaneously that they were hearing executions. Marson nodded at Asch, who was frowning, and then nodding, too. They were certain of it, now. The old man began to mutter, low, a singsong whose words were not even distinguishable as words.

"*Il mio paese*," he said to Marson. And he put his head down.

"*Paese.*"

"*Amici. Amici del mio cuore.*" The old man put one hand on his chest, over his heart.

"*Amici*—friend," Marson said. "Friend of your heart."

"*Casa mia.* How you say—house."

"Home."

"*Sì.*"

"I'm so sorry."

The old man did not respond. He folded his hands tightly at his thin chest, concentrating very deeply on something in his own thoughts, muttering low again.

"*Assassini,*" the old man said through his bad teeth. "Killers."

They listened and the shooting went on, slow, gaps of a few seconds between shots, a volley each time, a firing squad, and the Germans were apparently shooting a lot of people, lining them up and shooting them down. With each volley the old man uttered a little sound of grief.

"Goddamn," Asch said. "Are they shooting *everybody*?"

"*Vigliacchi. Criminali.*"

"They're shooting criminals?"

"*Sono criminali.*"

"I don't understand what the fuck he's saying," Asch said. "Are they shooting the whole village?"

"*I Tedeschi sono criminali,*" said the old man.

"The Germans are the criminals," Marson said.

"*Vigliacchi! Sì.* Cowards. *Tedeschi.*" He spit.

They listened. There were two more volleys, and then a pause, then two more. It went on.

"Goddamn," Asch said. "Goddamn."

There was a long pause. And then it began again.

Marson said, "What the hell."

"*God*damn them," Asch said suddenly, loud. "Oh, goddamn them." He stood and looked out over the mound of drifted snow at the marked wide field and the tops of trees and shouted, "You goddamn motherfucking sons of bitches! I'll kill every fucking one of you!"

"But who are they shooting?" Joyner said. "Are they killing the whole fucking village? What the fuck."

"*Ebrei*," said the old man.

"*Ebrei*," Asch said. "I heard that at Palermo. *Ebrei*. Hebrews. He's talking about Jews." He looked out at the marked-up snowfield, the black tops of the trees. "They're shooting Jews?"

They had heard rumors of what the Germans were doing in the north. They had not believed the rumors.

Joyner was digging at his arm, his mouth pulled back in a grimace.

"*Ebrei*," said the old man, looking down. "*Sì*."

Asch had even talked about atrocity propaganda from the first war, having heard similar stories from his grandfather.

"Why would they—?" Marson said. And his nausea came back, silencing him. He turned and sat down in the snow, leaning against the rock wall. Beside him, Asch's voice had spilled over into a kind of manic muttering.

"That's—that's bullshit. That's bullshit. They're shooting partisans. Something—"

"What the fuck," Joyner said. "What the *fuck*."

"*Ebrei*," the old man said. "*Amici*." His eyes kept brimming. "*Amici*."

They heard another volley. It made them all wince. Marson tried to pray, murmuring the Lord's Prayer. He kept repeating the phrase in his mind, *deliver us from evil, deliver us from evil . . .*

"That's bullshit," Asch said, again, and then again. And then he murmured something in another language: "*Yisgadal v'yiskadash sh'mei rabbaw.*" He took a quick, sobbing breath. "*B'allmaw dee v'raw chir'usei v'yamlich malchusei, b'cha-yeichon, uv'yomeichon, uv'chayei d'chol beis yisroel . . .*"

"What're you saying?" Joyner asked.

Asch looked at him as if he had been startled out of sleep. "Nothing," he said. "I don't believe it." He gestured with a tilting of his head toward the direction of the shots, the village. "But they do."

Joyner did not take his eyes away.

"It's called Kaddish, okay? Mourner's Prayer. Prayer for the dead."

Joyner sat back and began concentrating on his arm again. "Goddamn," he said. "Oh god*damn*."

"I learned it as a kid," Asch told them. Then he muttered again: "*Y'hei shlawmaw rabbaw min sh'mayaw, v'chayim awleinu v'al kol yisroel.*"

"What's it mean?" Marson asked him.

"Yeah," Joyner said, almost like a challenge, except that he had a forlorn look in his eyes. "Tell us what it's saying."

Asch sighed, and the tears ran down his cheeks. "Ah—God. Look. It means—I don't know what it means. It means you say it for the dead." He gasped, choked, held his fist to his mouth, then took it away—his hand dropped to his side. "It means whatever it means when you can't—" He sniffled and ran his wrist across his face. "Ah. Man," he said. "Words. God-damn."

They were all silent then. Asch murmured the prayer under his breath.

Each volley made them recoil. And it went on, and on. Perhaps an hour of it while they looked out at the snowfield with its tracks leading away. The sky above them was beautiful, dark and full of stars, with small white tufts and high thin ribbons of cirrus, gleaming at the edges with the moon. The whole sky was colored with that light, and the stars sparkled in it like gemstones strewn across a vast bed.

"What're you gonna report now about the Kraut whore?" Joyner said suddenly, low.

Asch didn't answer him for a moment. Then: "I'm gonna report a murder."

"No shit. After this?"

"Yes," Asch said. "*Especially* after this. *Especially* after this, goddamn it."

"She was a fucking Nazi, Saul. Christ. How clear do you need it to be?"

Another volley quieted them. Asch sat very still, staring

out. Then he was sick, putting his head down between his knees.

Marson watched him and kept trying to pray. He could not find the words. Each time there was a volley, the sound of it and what it meant rose up in him, facing at him, a wall against which his own soul could only collide in unbelief. He searched for something to feel other than the sickness and the vacancy of not being able to process the fact of what the sounds meant. It was all a blankness like the blankness of a field of snow where no human tracks have ever been made. And the world before his eyes *was* beautiful, like a painting, and the stars sparkled in the sky.

"Maybe they're shooting officers, like the guy back up the hill," Joyner said, and then seemed to choke.

Asch indicated the old man. "You heard him."

"Murderers," the old man said, distinctly, like someone well versed in the language. He looked at Marson and said it again, clearly. "Murderers."

"God," Marson said. "Ah, God."

In another moment, the volleys stopped. And the silence became freighted with waiting for the next one, which didn't come.

"I can't stand this anymore," Joyner said suddenly. He stood and hurled his carbine down into the snowfield—it made no sound, dropping in and leaving the imprint of itself—then ripped his field jacket off, and his blouse, so that his arms were bare. He knelt and stuck his bad arm down in the snow, all the way to the shoulder.

"Joyner, for Christ's sweet sake," Asch said, wiping the back of his hand across his face, sniffling.

Joyner didn't move, but kept the arm down in the snow, the whole arm.

"Come on, Joyner," said the corporal. "Don't make me have to report you."

"Hey, don't report me. Shoot me."

"Stop this. Get your gear and your stuff together. We're moving out."

They waited. He wept a little, moving the bad arm in the snowdrift, as if he had lost something and was feeling around for it. Finally he stood again and wiped the snow from himself, crying, cursing. Asch handed him his shirt. Asch buttoned it for him because in the few moments the snow had rendered Joyner's hand too numb to function. He let it dangle at his side while Asch worked on him.

"I gotta get off this fucker," Joyner said. "Jesus Christ. We gotta get away from all this shit. It's shit. I gotta get back off this motherfucker of a mountain and out of this fucking terrible place."

Marson said, "Go get your weapon."

"I don't care what you tell them down on the road. I don't care if they court-martial me. Fuck it. I mean it."

"Let's just get this over with, Joyner. Okay?"

Joyner walked out onto the snowfield and made his way across to the weapon. And he brought it back, head down. He stood with the others, carbine in one hand, scratching that forearm with the other hand.

"Let's go," Marson said.

"I'm staying here," said Joyner, still looking down. "I'll be here when you come back through. And I don't care what you do and I don't care what you say."

Marson waited.

"Near," the old man said, low. It was clear that he had understood what was happening.

"Joyner, don't do this," Marson said.

"I'll cover your back, Corporal. I'm not going over there."

Marson felt an urge, nearly irresistible, to strike him. But they were in this space together now, having been through the sounds from the village, having been faced with this some-thing so far beyond their own worst expectations of them-selves or of the world, even a world at war. It was a strange, sorrowful moment, suffused almost with a tenderness. He had to work to put it down in himself. He took a breath, and then turned to Asch. "You're a witness to this," he said. He was calling it up from all his training. "And I believe the penalty for desertion is death."

Asch looked at him with unconcealed surprise.

"Got it?" Marson said.

"It's not desertion if I'm covering your back," said Joyner, a pleading note in his voice.

"It's desertion if you disobey an order to march in a combat situation."

"*È molto vicino.* Good—near."

"Tell him to shut up," Joyner said. "Goddamn it, I mean it. I don't like his language. Tell him to just shut the fuck up."

"I'm telling *you* to shut up," Marson said. And he turned to Asch again. "You're a witness."

"I'm that," said Asch. "I *am* that—Christ."

"We're going on," Marson said to Joyner. "You can stay here and suffer the consequences or you can fall in. If you fall in, we never mention it." He gestured for Angelo to lead on, and started with him around the snow mound, descending again. After a few paces, he stopped. Asch and Joyner were coming behind them.

"*Molto vicino,*" the old man said.

They kept going. Not talking, following him. There were no openings in the trees, and the ground kept dipping. They kept descending. You couldn't see out for the tree branches, all pines now, thick and drooping with snow. The air was colder on this side of the mountain, or seemed so. At last they came to a shoulder, at the end of which they could see a narrow plain, opening out below, with the river running far off to the left, and the road and several farm fields ending in the cluster of buildings and houses that was, no doubt, Angelo's unfortunate village. Beyond that were foothills and the other mountains. On the road, going away, several tanks rolled along, panzers, and, looking through the scope, you could see the troops marching alongside them. It looked like an orderly retreat.

NINETEEN

T HEY HAD TURNED AROUND and were climbing
    again, going back up to the crest, past the marks of their
descending. They got to the snowfield in front of the long ter-
racelike ledge, and when Saul Asch paused to adjust a damp
fold in the front of his field jacket, something hit him in the
back.

As he toppled forward, they all heard the shot.

It came from very far off. Asch went over like a felled tree.
The others scurried for the drift of snow under the ledge.
They made it there and got down and stayed down, and
waited. Marson looked out over the snow hillock. Asch lay still
and quiet, on his stomach in the open, face to one side.

"Jesus, Jesus, Jesus, Jesus," Joyner kept saying under his
breath. The old man moaned and lay on his side, his cloak
pulled high over his head.

"Where'd it come from?" Marson said.

"I don't know," Joyner said. "Christ. Behind us. Way off."

"A sniper?"

"Oh, Jesus, Jesus, Jesus. I knew it. They're following us."

"No, it's a sniper."

"Are you sure?" Joyner sighted with his carbine, sweeping the panorama of the moonlit space.

Out in the field, Asch moved, seemed about to try and get up. Marson called to him. "Stay absolutely still, Saul. Don't move. If he knows you're alive he'll shoot again. Hold still!"

Joyner said, "We can't leave him there."

"Shut up, we're not going to."

"He'll die if we don't get to him."

The moon shone, terribly bright in a mostly clear and starry sky, and Asch's shape in the field was not moving. Everything beyond him looked as still as a photograph.

Joyner became worried that the enemy could be working around the snowfield in the trees. He kept thinking he heard footfalls, and twice he whirled, ready to shoot.

"I'm telling you it's a sniper," Marson said.

The old man repeated the word in English. Then moaned and crossed himself. Marson looked out at Asch where he lay, a shadow outlined with silver light. There was so much light. It hurt the eyes to look at it. But there were little moving silvery clouds in the sky. A small tuft was drifting slow on a trajectory to block the moon. It might cover it, or part of it, for a little space. "I'm coming to get you, Asch. Just stay still."

They waited. The little cloud missed the moon. The old

man whimpered and seemed again to be saying something, some chant in Italian, repeating it over and over. The cold felt solid now, the wind battering them. "I'm gonna go get him," Marson said.

"Jesus, do you think he's dead?"

"I'm not leaving him there."

"I didn't say that," Joyner got out. And then he seemed to think more deeply into what had been said. "Hey, fuck you, Marson."

"Just stay put," Marson told him. "When I start, cover me."

"Cover you how? The fucker's probably on another mountain."

They peered at the snowfield and the trees beyond, trying to decide where the shot must have come from. Because there had been no more shooting, they knew this was indeed a sniper, a straggler left behind to delay pursuit. And probably he was still out there somewhere.

The wind lifted more snow, and as a cloud shadow passed across the field, Marson got to his feet, his legs trembling as with some nerve weakness, and made for where Asch lay. He took one shaky step, and then another, and another. He felt as though he might collapse any second. The moon, even in the little fold of cloud, was still dazzling, the field too bright, and there were all the foot tracks of human progress across it, and he thought of it that way—oddly, like a reflection in someone else's mind, even while he ran, even while he felt the terror and the certainty of eyes on him—that here were the signs of human habitation in the open snowy expanse, as if it were the surface of some ice planet. It seemed to him that the stars beyond the clouds and the moon were making their own light. He pushed through the crusting snow, wishing for perfect darkness, feeling himself exposed, watched, followed in sights, a figure in crosshairs, moving in a zigzag, expecting any moment to feel the piercing of the bullet, and to feel it before the sound reached him. But he got to Asch and pitched forward in the snow, his face only inches from Asch's face.

Asch lay quite still, eyes closed, the snow adhering to his cheeks. His mouth was slightly open, and snow had got into it. Crystals of it glistened in his hair. Marson thought of the dead German. He reached over and got Asch's helmet, which had flown from him when he fell.

"Saul," he said, into the snow-spattered face.

Asch opened his eyes. "I'm shot," he said. "Christ." He started to cry. "Oh, Jesus Christ. I'm shot."

"Listen to me," Marson said. "Can you get up?"

The other man gave him a look of profound exasperation. "Yeah. You wanna dance? We'll waltz out of here. They'll never know what happened."

"If I put your arm over my neck, can you help walk?"

"Just get me out of here, man. I'm shot. Goddamn. I'm shot. Oh, Jesus Christ." He was crying again.

Marson got to his knees, shouldered Asch's carbine alongside his own, and then lifted him, standing, using his hip and managing to get the other's arm across his own neck while still holding the helmet. He staggered with the weight, calling on what felt like the last of his strength, trying to run, aware that snipers watched for the ones trying to help. He felt the immense certainty that he would be shot in the next instant. It made his bowels drop. His voice went out from him, a cry, like a cry of pain. But nothing struck. He was struggling with the other man in the moonlit field and nothing came from the shooter in the distance.

"I can't feel my fucking legs, man." Asch sobbed. "I'll never see my child, you know? Christ. I'm gonna die now, right? Isn't that right, Marson? I'm gonna die. Oh, Christ, I can't feel my legs."

Marson carried him, stumbling in the heavy snow, toward the protection of the ledge, beyond the hillock of driven snow with their frantic tracks all over it. The knowledge that he would not hear the shot until it hit him made him groan and push through, panic rising in him, the sound of the snow breaking at his feet too loud, everything pounding, everything shouting with the not-sound of the bullet he felt coming at him, and he was down at last, out of the clearing at last, below the level of the hill, under the ledge, gasping, and Joyner crouched there with the old man, both of them staring out at the place from which he and Asch had come. There were no other shots.

TWENTY

JOYNER PUT A BLANKET DOWN in a flat dry place
under the ledge. Asch lay partly on his right side. He
moaned, half conscious now. The other two worked on him,
removing his pack and pulling at his field jacket and blouse to
get a look at the wound. The bullet had entered his rib cage,
missing bone, about eight to ten inches above his hip on the
left side, and exited a little down from that and perhaps an
inch toward the middle of his lower abdomen. It had traveled
a long way and did not seem to have broken bone. The exit
wound was slightly larger than the entrance wound, and the
blood kept coming there, a spreading black stain in the moonlight. Joyner and Marson kept trying to stanch it with gauzes
from Marson's first-aid kit, and then from Joyner's. They
pressed their hands to it, and Marson worried about what
might be approaching from the other side of the field. But the
old man was watching, and also watching the struggle to stop
Asch's bleeding.

"I'm freezing," Asch said. "I'm so fucking cold."

Marson tried to cover him, but you couldn't work to stop the bleeding if you couldn't see the wounds, and now the entrance wound began bleeding, too, filling with blood and then flowing over. The blanket was soaked. They kept working the wounds.

"It's not stopping," Asch sobbed. "Christ. I'm emptying out."

"It is stopping," Joyner told him. "It is."

They worked on, feeling the inimical presence in the moon-haunted dark all around them.

"I didn't do anything," Asch said, low, beginning to cry. "I was a nice guy. I never hurt anybody intentionally, I swear it."

"Shut up," said Joyner. "It's stopping. We'll wrap you up and take you down and you'll be out of the fuck'n war."

"I'm scared, Benny. It's bad, isn't it. I can't stop shivering."

Joyner was silent, working hard to make the bleeding stop. Marson stood and looked out at the field and the sky. Asch's breathing was becoming faster. The entrance wound had stopped bleeding. Another blast of the wind made him realize that the man's bare flesh was exposed. He knelt and tried to cover his back with the bloody field jacket. Joyner was still working the exit wound, murmuring, "It's slowing down. Slowing down now. It's gonna be fine. It's stopping."

"It's starting to hurt," Asch said. "Oh, Christ help me. It hurts bad."

"It's stopped bleeding," Joyner said. "The cold's good. It's really slowing it down."

"I'm freezing. God."

"It's doing good. Almost completely stopped now. I swear."

"I need something for the pain, though. Give me something for the pain."

There were morphine syringes in the first-aid kit. Marson pulled the seal from one and stuck it into Asch's thigh.

"Give him another one," Joyner said.

Marson did so.

"I didn't mean anything," Asch moaned.

The corporal saw Angelo watching all of this, and watching the field, too. The old man's face looked changed, the odd marks in the forehead showing in the shadowy light, the black eyes simply taking everything in. Marson had an unpleasant foreboding sense of having missed something about him.

Asch wept softly, apologizing for the noise. "I didn't mean anything. I'm sorry, fellas."

"You're out of the war," Joyner said. "You lucky son of a bitch."

"But God, Benny. There's so much blood."

"We've all got gallons of it," Joyner told him. "Plenty to spare. I bled as much from a head cut in a football game."

"I got it all over," said Asch as if worried about the mess.

"It's stopping," Joyner told him. "You take a vial of blood you'd donate and spill it and it'll look about like this."

"I spilled a lot of blood, fellas." Asch sobbed.

For a little space, then, they were all quiet. There was only the sound of the wounded soldier's breathing and moaning. "If I could quit shivering. God—I knew we'd get it. I knew it.

I knew we'd get it on this fucking piece-of-shit mountain. We were cursed from the start."

Through it all, the old man seemed simply to regard the others in their trouble while continuing to keep watch on the snowfield. It seemed to Marson that he had the demeanor of someone who had no fear for himself anymore. He seemed almost detached. It was disturbing, and Marson marked it, deciding that it would be wise to watch him more closely. It was possible that instead of keeping watch for an approaching enemy, he was looking for a possible rescuer. The thought blew through the corporal like a blast of icy wind, and he stepped over to the old man and looked out at the field. "Do you see something?" he asked. *"Capeesh?"*

The old man shook his head. Something about him appeared faintly arrogant now, as if he could not be bothered to fear or respect these armed boys he was with in their trouble. Marson thought of this and it was as if he were briefly inside the other's mind. He stood close, trying to see into the darkness of the eyes. The moon did not lend enough light to see the irises. But Marson was reasonably certain that he was not imagining the feeling. He said, *"Tedesco?"*

"Italiano, signore."

"Guide, right?"

"Guida, sì."

"Tedeschi out there?" Marson pointed.

"Tedeschi—no. *Nessun tedesco. Nessuno che vede. Niente."*

"You take us back down this mountain." Corporal Marson wanted it to have the force of a command.

But the old man looked at him blankly and seemed to be waiting for him to falter somehow. *"Non capisco."*

"Fellas?" Asch said suddenly. "Fellas?"

"We're here," Joyner told him.

"Fellas, I can't move my legs."

"I'm sure it missed your spine," Joyner said.

"I can't move my legs, fellas."

Joyner grabbed his ankle. "Can you feel that?"

"Feel what?"

He looked at Marson.

"Oh, Christ—Christ. I can't feel my legs."

"It'll pass," Joyner told him. He was still working the exit wound. Marson watched the old man, and the trees. He used the scope to pan the expanse of disturbed snow and the far tree line. He saw no movement anywhere.

"You're gonna be thanking God for this wound," Joyner said to Asch.

He got the bleeding stopped at last. But there was still the problem of the legs. It was strange that the legs were as they were, since the bullet had missed the spine altogether, by several inches. It had exited on a line inches to the left side. Nothing of it would have broken off or splintered. There was no danger of injuring the spine with motion, or there wasn't any that Marson could think of, and Joyner, who Stateside had done a few weeks of training as a medic, said there certainly wasn't. Joyner attributed the loss of feeling to shock and said he was practically certain feeling would return as soon as Asch's blood pressure rose to normal. He said as much to

Asch, speaking with certainty, and Asch thanked him, and then lapsed into semiconsciousness. "Billy?" he said, loud, so that his voice carried. "Where's the toothpaste. Somebody took the toothpaste."

Joyner said, "I've got it, Saul."

Asch seemed greatly relieved. "Ah, thanks, Billy. You're a good brother." He wept a little more. "I should've given you that baseball glove. You should've seen what I saw, Billy. In the Sahara Desert. Can't get it out of my mind." Joyner was working to get the bandages tight around the wound.

They could not be certain there was no internal bleeding. From this angle, it looked like the bullet could have perforated part of the bowel. Joyner leaned into Marson and told him this. Marson saw the old man watching them.

"Father?" Asch said, low, and was gone again.

They wrapped him in bandages from all three kits. The old man watched them and kept glancing at the row of trees bordering the field on the right side.

"You waiting for something there?" Marson asked him again.

The old man did not know he was being addressed.

"Angelo."

He turned, startled.

"Anything you're expecting to see out there?"

"*Non capisco,*" Angelo said.

They closed Asch's field jacket, and after a wait of a few tense minutes, scanning the prospect of the field in the bath of moonlight and the trees lining it, they began again their trek across the brow of the mountain and toward the way down. Marson carried Asch over his back, holding one arm at the wrist and, with his left hand through the legs, gripping the thick thigh. Joyner carried the carbines and two packs. The old man led them, carrying the other pack. They moved through the trees. Several times they had to stop and listen, and rest. They made very slow progress. And all the time the air got colder, the wind more piercing. They kept moving, and Marson's legs burned, his sides caught, he couldn't breathe out fully. The blister on his heel sent white-hot pain all the way to his hip. He would stagger the few feet to the next tree, the next shape or outcropping of rock that might provide cover from a distant shooter, and he continued trying to pray, the God he believed in beginning to feel like the immensity itself all around him. And through it all, he kept sensing someone trying to hold him in crosshairs.

When they arrived at the site of the camp with the dead German in it, they got to the other side of the downed tree and tried to rest awhile. Marson set Asch down carefully in the snow, so that he lay partly on his side again. Joyner looked to see if the wounds were bleeding more. They were not. The two soldiers ranged themselves on either side of Asch and breathed the cold air, and waited for the strength to continue. Asch was unconscious, dreaming something. He mentioned Billy several times, and Africa, in a jumble of words. Marson did not want to think that in his delirium he might be reliving the burning tank.

The wind picked up again, but the snow had mostly frozen,

a crust of solidness that their boots had to break through with each step they took. It had drifted over the body of the German officer almost entirely—the body made only a human-shaped mound, now, with a little sharp corner of frozen cloth, a shirt collar, jutting out of it where the neck would be.

Marson drank from his canteen and realized the old man was watching him. He offered the canteen, and the old man drank deeply. If the sniper was pursuing them, he could pick them off one by one. The thought brought Marson to a crouch, peering out past the body-shaped mound, for any sign of movement. The old man handed him the canteen and got down behind the tree, knees up, arms wrapped around them.

"I don't think we'll ever know who it was or what it was," Joyner said.

"They send stragglers," Marson said. "He probably shot once and went on with the retreat."

"Or he's fuck'n hunting us."

Marson looked out. The trees and shadows appeared motionless as printed images. The wind had paused.

"It's not so bad, the cold, as long as the wind isn't blowing." Joyner offered his canteen to Asch, who had stirred but had not quite awakened. He took it back and drank of it, little sips, and then he made a gagging noise. "Sorry," he said.

"You all right?" Marson asked him.

"I'm sick. It was a lot of blood. I don't do blood too well, you know? I couldn't make it through medic training because of it."

The field, which looked like a lane between the two rows of trees, was unchanged. "What time do you think it is?"

"Not much past midnight."

The old man coughed and sputtered and rubbed his mouth. He laid his head back against the tree and closed his eyes.

"I've got an idea," Joyner said.

Marson turned to him.

"Let's set the Kraut up to look like one of us, with a carbine. Lean him against the tree or something. If there's a sniper on our tail, maybe he'll take a shot at our dead friend. You know? It can be a warning for us."

Marson said, "What if he shoots us while we're setting it up?"

"We're in some tree shade here. Be a tough shot."

"You want to take that chance?"

"If there's something I can do to get rid of the feeling somebody's drawing a fuck'n bead on me all the way down this fucker."

"Okay, then let's do it."

They stood at the same time, and the old man stood, too. Marson noticed that he had put Asch's pack on, and the straps hung from it. Probably it provided some warmth for him. When Marson tried to catch his eye, to communicate, the old man simply looked away.

"No move," Corporal Marson said. "Stay."

The old man waited. Marson stepped over to him and gestured for him to get down. Asch moaned and then turned slightly and raised his head. "Robert?"

"We're gonna set up a decoy," Marson said to him.

"We're not down the mountain?"

"Not yet."

"I knew it. I'm bleeding again, too. I can feel it."

Marson knelt down, pulled back the field jacket, and looked at the bandaged place. He saw no stain of blood on it. "You're not bleeding now," he said.

"I can feel it," said Asch. "Inside."

"Stay still," Marson said, and again he gestured to the old man to get down. Joyner had already moved to the other side of the tree, had already stepped into the water of the little stream, which the snow had covered. It had not quite frozen over. He cursed and sat down. "Fuck'n ice. Goddamn it. I'll get frostbite now and lose a fuck'n foot."

Marson walked over and helped him stand. They stood on the other side of the tree, in the moonlight, and they realized it at the same time, looking out along the snow lane, fearing the shot they would not hear.

TWENTY-ONE

I T TOOK A LONG TIME, working to free the corpse, breaking the frozen crust with their entrenching tools, and then scooping at the snow with their hands to get to the outline of it. Ice had formed over the face, and the hands had frozen so solidly that the fingers would not come free. Joyner chopped through four of the fingers with the sharp end of the tool to free the left hand. He gagged and coughed, moving off a few feet, to the trees. He kept gasping. "This is awful," he said. "Goddamn."

"Come on," said Marson.

"I'm sick."

The old man coughed and moved out from the tree, holding Asch's pack. "*Che cosa state facendo?* What that you do?"

"Down," Marson said to him, gesturing.

Joyner made his way back to the body and began tearing at the snow around the legs. He kept muttering, cursing, glancing at the open space in its bath of lunar brightness. Marson got down to help him, and the old man simply crouched and watched them.

Somehow they got the other hand free without damaging it. Twice they stopped, and listened, and Joyner went and checked on Asch, who was by turns fitfully awake and unconscious. The old man went back to the tree trunk and sat against it, with Asch's pack behind him for a cushion. He rocked back and forth in the cold, arms clasping his upraised knees, staring at Asch, and intermittently he would raise himself and fix his gaze on the open area of ground.

The body was rock solid, stiff, and much heavier than either of the two soldiers imagined it could be. Finally the old man had to come around the tree and help. They got it upright, but the arms were outstretched, as though it were reaching for the clear, star- and moon-bright sky. The shadow it made across the trampled surface of snow looked like the shadow of a statue. "I never thought I'd ever wish for rain," Joyner said. "Something other than this fuck'n moon. Jesus."

They lifted the body like a big solid log, carried it to one of the trees just beyond the campsite, and propped it there. Marson broke through the crust of snow and piled some of it around the feet for support. There were about eleven inches between the feet, the legs having spread slightly in the toppling over from being shot.

"Nobody's gonna be fooled by this," Joyner wheezed. He stood there trying to gain his breath back.

"Can we get the arms down?"

"Solid as stone."

"Wrap your blanket roll around him."

"Have to use Asch's. Mine's covered with blood."

Asch's was also covered with blood, and stiffening in the cold. They got it to conform to the shape of the body. Then they stepped back a little to look at it in the dimness. It looked as though the soldier were trying to climb the tree.

"Let's wrap the blanket around the arms and the tree," Marson said, "and leave the head out."

They tried this. Joyner was gasping for air and coughing, gagging. Marson kept track of the old man out of the corner of his eye. When they got the body tied, they stepped back again to survey their work. Now it looked as though the figure were hugging the tree.

"Shit," Joyner said. "It's gonna have to do."

Marson put Asch's helmet on it. He had to pack the helmet with snow. Joyner emptied the clip from Asch's carbine and lay it in the fold of the blanket near the chest line. Through it all they had to keep pausing to listen.

"Well," Marson said, gazing at it. "I don't know."

"It looks like a stiff tied to a fuck'n tree."

"A mannequin," Marson said. "But maybe from a distance."

Asch made a noise of choking, and they hurried around to him. Saliva had gathered in the back of his throat. He coughed it up, looked at them, muttered something about the cold, and began to murmur, crying. They couldn't make any of it out. Then he lapsed back into unconsciousness.

Marson stationed himself near the base of the tree and scoped the lane between the rows of trees. Joyner sat beside him with his back to the trunk. The old man faced Joyner, crouched low, gazing at Asch, who kept twitching and moaning, but did not come to. Marson felt the searing pain in his foot. He waited for the strength to move. There were more clouds now, a wide shoreline-looking expanse of them, advancing incrementally from the east. Soon it would be as dark as it had been in the rain. Marson indicated this to Joyner, who nodded.

They got Asch across Joyner's back, and with the old man carrying Asch's pack, they started again, making their way slowly, torturously down, and Marson did not remember it being this steep at this part of the climb. But the snow held them some, the crust of it breaking with each stride they made and then hugging their thighs. The old man took them back down the path on which he'd first led them, and at one bend in it, he paused, and looked to his left, expectation on his face. He peered through the trees.

"You see something?" Marson asked him.

"*Niente*." But there had been that look.

When they came to the place where they had seen the buck, they moved to the lee of a big tree and paused again. Asch remained unconscious but breathing. The old man put the pack down and leaned on it, sighing.

Marson looked at him, certain that there had been a subtle change in him; now he seemed like someone full of anticipation. His manner was that of a man waiting in ambush.

"Angelo," Marson told him, smiling. "If you do anything to guide them to us I'll shoot you before I take the first shot at them. *Capeesh?*"

"Guida," the old man said, nodding. He smiled but then seemed to think better of it. He had his arms wrapped about himself, leaning against Asch's pack.

"I said from the start I don't trust him." Joyner was winded. His words came with a rasping. "Christ. He'd do it, too. You see it now, too. Right? You think he's Fascist, too."

"I don't know what I think," Marson said.

"Non sono fascista," said Angelo.

They waited. Joyner drank from his canteen and then, after a hesitation that demonstrated his distrust, offered it to the old man, who had just put a handful of snow in his mouth. The old man shook his head. *"Grazie,* no."

In the next half minute of silence they heard a shot, echoing across the silent snow and the blackness of the trees, from very far.

TWENTY-TWO

Sound carries farther at this height, Marson told himself. The shot was behind them. He believed it had come from there. "I'm going to double back," he told Joyner. "And take him out."

"Naw, look," Joyner said. "Let's just get back down off this fucker."

"We can't move fast enough. He'll pick us off. He'll get where he can see us all and he'll pick us off."

"I don't think so. I think we should get down to the road fast."

Marson thought a moment. "Let Angelo take you down. Just keep going. I'll catch up to you either way."

The old man stared from one to the other of them. But then he pointed back up the mountain. "*Tedeschi,*" he said.

"Yeah. Get going," Marson said.

Asch moaned.

"This cold will save his life," Joyner said. "He can't bleed like he would in warmer conditions, I know that."

"Get him down this mountain. I mean it. I'll follow. I can follow the snow trail."

Joyner shook his head. "I got a bad feeling."

"We've gotta know anyway what's trailing us. If it's a regiment, they'll need to know down on the road, right?"

"It's a sniper. I think he probably won't come much farther."

"Just do this for me," Marson said. "Take Asch and go." He looked at the old man. "Down the mountain. *Capeesh?*"

"*Sì,*" the old man said. But clearly he did not understand anything, and only meant to show his loyalty.

Marson indicated Asch, and Joyner, and then he pointed down the mountain. "*Guida.*"

"Oh," the old man said, almost eagerly. "*Sì.* Yes. Yes."

"Sorry," Asch mumbled, not quite conscious.

"Okay, we're going down," Joyner said to the old man. "You take one false move and you're dead. *Morto. Capeesh?*"

Angelo looked frightened.

Marson indicated the direction, and gestured again. "Down."

"*Sì.* Yes."

He moved off. The old man watched him go. Joyner was doing something with Asch, and Marson saw that he had removed Asch's watch. He went on, wending slowly back through the trees, keeping to the right of the path and going from tree to tree, skirting the ground they had already covered but remaining within clear sight of it, moving very slowly, stopping frequently to listen to the woods. Around him the moonlight began to fail, the shoreline-bright mass of cloud having come over, thin at first, so that the moon shone behind it, but thickening, darkening. The woods seemed more dense in the gloom. At one point it came over him like revelation that he was in Italy, alone, in woods, in the middle of the longest night of his life, and there was someone out there with a scope rifle, hunting him. He stood against a big tree, breathing the odor of its heavy bark, and thought of the pain in his heel. It hurt worse all the time, and yet he could not quite get his mind around it as pain. This that he felt now, stalking the dark, expecting every second to be shot, this was the kind of strain that overmastered the physical discomforts he was suffering, and there was still the cold, the freeze at his fingertips and at the ends of his toes, the shivering, and the feeling of wanting simply to lie down and rest, even knowing that to rest was to die. He could not conjure the slightest image of his own life before this moment, this black quiet, with the terror of any motion or sound, and the sting in his lungs, the shakiness of the muscles in his lower back and his legs.

All for thee, most sacred heart of Jesus.

The words had no meaning. There existed nothing anymore but these woods, this deep stillness. His senses were sharper than they had ever been, and yet he could not think of anything but the darkness and what could be hiding in it. He moved in the blackness like a cat, searching for a place to wait in ambush.

He came to within a few yards of the campsite and saw the corpse lying next to the tree. This fact thrilled him. He got down on his knees, behind a stone outcropping, and waited. After a few minutes of listening, and panning the lane with the scope, he got to where he could see the corpse, but he could not tell in the dark if there had been a hit. He was a few feet away from the downed tree's root system, and he got below the line of it, moving closer to the slight depression in the snow where the fire had been. It had grown too dark to be sure of anything. He simply waited now, reasonably certain that a bullet had knocked the corpse over—the ruse had worked perfectly—and the corpse must have dropped like a shot man. The sniper, if he were indeed following, would then come forward, keeping his distance, moving with the deliberateness of his kind. It felt that way to Marson, as if he were seeking to stop some species, a creature occurring in nature.

The dark was nearly complete. The possibility existed that the sniper had moved beyond this little square of ground, and so it was necessary to try watching in all directions. Marson turned slowly, looking through the almost useless scope. The sense that the sniper may have got by him fed his terror. And it was terror: a deep, black, nerve-tic distress so pervasive that it was hardly aware of itself. Marson stared out at the night in a freezing, fixed gaze of expectation. The darkness yielded no sound. The wind had died. The air grew colder all the time. The line of trees, left and right, the open lane, all of it seemed to be fading out of existence as light left the sky.

Once or twice, over the next minutes, he believed that the corpse moved, or sighed, or took in air. His mind began playing tricks on him. He saw another deer and almost shot at it. The sound of the hooves piercing the snow crust startled him so badly that he let go a little cry from the bottom of his throat. The deer went on. The woods grew silent again. The cold changed in increments of freezing, everything turning to ice. The condensation of his breath froze on his lips. He was beginning to believe that the night would yield up nothing and this had all been a waste. Certainly Joyner and the old man must be well down the mountain, with their cargo. He saw in his mind the look on Asch's face as the bleeding went on, and he knew he should feel sorry for him. He *had* felt sorry for him, and for everyone in the world. But he did not feel it now. He could not find any sense of Asch as another someone. It was as if he were an idea, only a word on someone's lips, a concept. In his mind's eye, he saw the little cracked photograph of his own daughter, and it meant nothing to him. It was a photograph, insubstantial as thought. The waiting was changing him, emptying him, draining all the human elements, as if his spirit were bleeding. He tried to picture Helen, his father and mother, the street, the *surround*, as he had seen it on that last day. He could not call it up. He could not begin to imagine it. The memory of it all was breaking up, dissolving, being effaced awfully. He could see quite clearly the eyes filled with wonder of the dying soldier, the woman's smudged calves. He had become a pair of eyes, staring, two hands on a rifle. A cold watchfulness, shivering in the wind, waiting.

He had not really thought through how he would proceed when he encountered the sniper, what sort of action he might take. He did not know if he was capable of a shot from ambush, and this would have to be just that. He tried imagining himself through it, as he had often imagined himself through pitching to one hitter or another, when he was a good baseball player and there were stupid, trivial things to worry about. He could not see himself through it. He tried to call up the longing he had felt to have his life back again, and he had felt it for so long, and that was gone, too, now. He told himself that he would never complain about anything in his life, if he could take his life out of here, home from this cold dark country with its hills and valleys and mountains, its bad weather. But these were just words, just noises in the mind.

And sleep began to come over him, with stealth, like a kind of nerve-killing predator, closing him down. He nodded off once, caught himself, straightened a little and tightened his grip on the carbine, then nodded off again. His head came against the rough bark of a thick root, and he jolted awake, amazed at the power of this drowsiness, even knowing that he could pay for it with his life. His eyelids were so heavy, so heavy. He took a handful of the snow and put it on his face, felt the intense sting of it, trying to recover his senses. And very quickly the drowse began again. He knelt and pulled at tendrils of the tree's root system, for exercise. Again, he put snow on his face. He saw himself standing in the clearing, and the deer were all around him, and he was falling far.

He woke almost shouting, holding the whimper back. The field had not changed. The night had not changed. He did not know how long he had been asleep, or if indeed he *had* been asleep, until he remembered the deer surrounding him, and the wide clearing he had stood in.

He had no sense of time, and now he had no sense of how long he had been watching the slow progress of a darker shape in the darkness, about a hundred yards from the little campsite, coming along just at the line of the trees, with the open snowfield to the right. He looked at the figure through the scope, but the glass was fogged now. He attempted to spit on the lens but could not produce enough saliva, so he put it in the snow and wiped it off, then raised it and found that he had lost the shape. He tried to see it again in the darkness and could not find it. He was ready to believe that he had been mistaken about what he saw, that it had been nothing more than another deer. He scanned the field again, the line of trees, and saw no moving thing. He put the scope down, and stared. Nothing. He waited, and felt the sleepiness again, and then saw motion, unmistakable, like the darkness itself moving. But it was a shape *in* the darkness, and he was immediately wide awake. It was no deer.

TWENTY-THREE

T HE MAN SEEMED faintly unconcerned with what might be waiting for him, though he was paying some attention to the darker places in the trees. His attitude was that of someone being cautious without fully believing that caution was necessary.

Marson carefully, as soundlessly as he could, attached the scope to his carbine, then got to his knees behind the downed tree, and drew a bead on him.

Not quite gradually, but with a sensation of a slow widening of himself, he felt a lessening of tension, as if something had been released in his blood, a drug, preventing him from feeling what he had felt only seconds before. In his mind he saw, in no order but in jumbled images, the Kraut dying, the soldier with the burned hand, Asch lying in the snow bleeding out of the little holes, the legs of the dead woman, the scenes of carnage going back to Salerno—and it was all one thing, cold in him, ice at the heart, something dead as the stone where he lay. He himself was stone, a statue's eyes looking out of dead granite, sighting along the barrel of the carbine, as he knew the sniper had done. Everything he had ever been, everything he had ever believed in or hoped for, and all his memories of home—they were all gone, elsewhere, obliterated in the freezing darkness of this pass, drawing the crosshairs over the figure approaching, and feeling his own finger tightening on the trigger. He could not shoot. He let go of the trigger, brought the carbine down to his side, watching the shape come on. He experienced a tremendous urge to look upon the face, but then thought of the place where he was, this place he had come to in his life. It felt, in some wordless way, like a whole life that he had only begun to live.

He raised the carbine again, sighted, and fired.

The shot went off into the night, echoing far, and the figure dropped over, was still. Marson waited, believing that there might be others, that another figure, other figures, would come, and he would shoot whoever tried to help the one down, and he realized that he was now, himself, a sniper.

But no one came. Nothing stirred. The shape lay in the snow, perhaps a hundred yards away, quite still.

Marson did not know how long he waited. But finally he got to his feet, edged forward, running at a crouch to the next tree, keeping to the tree line. When he came level with the shape, he waited a few more minutes, then stepped toward it, feeling the wind that had risen, as if it were an opposing force. He felt that his mind had never been more clean, nor more empty. He had the sense, again without words, that life—all life, the life he had led and the life he had come to—had never been so suffused with clarity, a terrible inhuman clarity, made utterly out of precision, like the precision of gear and tackle in a machine. Except that he understood, in a sick wave, that this was utterly and only human. He walked a few paces away and retched onto the snow. He looked at the thickly darkened sky and the field and experienced an over-powering sense of this as the world, the only world. He walked back to the still form lying there in the snow. In the dark of the field, he looked at the man he had killed, and was surprised to see that it was not a German soldier but an Ital-ian, with rope-soled shoes and a German officer's coat over him against the cold. Probably the coat that had not been with the body of the dead officer who had served as a decoy. And this was just a bandit, a killer moving among the armies. The face was dark, thin, heavy jawed, bearded, with high cheek-bones and a narrow cut of a mouth. Something lay on one of the black-whiskered cheeks, and Marson saw that it was a tooth, a molar, with its little extensions of bone. It made him sick again to see it. He moved the jaw, closed it. He took the sniper's scoped rifle away and threw it off into the snowfield. It was just him now, and the dead. Corporal Marson looked again at the open space and the tree line. This was the sniper. The rifle he had was scoped. It was the one.

He stumbled back out of the clearing and headed down to catch up with the others, moving quickly, as if running away from what he had just done. He was certain that he would not overtake them. He did not feel sick now, so much, but empty. It seemed that all the human parts of him had gone, had leeched out of him. He took a step and said his own name, and then said it again. It was just hollow sound. He knew nothing but the bitter cold and the silent woods, his own feet breaking through the crust of snow, the pain in his foot, the distant memory of a street and a house, a pregnant woman. "Do your duty," his father had said. And he could not find in his heart what the word meant anymore. Nothing meant anything. The particulars were all broken. Every single unabstract thing he thought glared at him, like an accusation. And "Do your duty" was an abstraction, and the dead made it seem ugly and irrelevant. Yet there was only the cold, and the way down, the trees bending with the weight of snow, the beautiful complications of windfall and rock and drifting that shaped the winter scene he moved through, and anyone would have said it was beautiful to see. He was alive, walking, breathing, remembering, and he had a deadness at his heart's core, a numbness, a sense of all his being having been reduced to a kind of obliterating concentration on this slow progress down the mountain.

He found Joyner and the old man and Asch not very far from where he had left them. Joyner challenged him, crouched behind a tree.

"It's me," Marson said, and felt as though he had lied. "Why haven't you gone farther than this?"

"Saul woke up and was sick. We couldn't move him," Joyner said. "I didn't want to leave you anyway, and you wouldn't either and you know it."

The old man stood there shivering, staring at Marson.

"We heard the shot," Joyner said. "I've never been so fuck'n spooked. I kept thinking what if it was you that got it."

"No."

"So you got him?"

Marson looked at the old man. "It wasn't a Jerry."

Joyner said, "What?"

"It was an Italian."

The old man said, "*Italiano?*"

"Yeah. *Italiano.*" Marson turned his carbine on the old man, who held his hands toward him.

"*Un certo figlio d'una puttana fascista.* Some on a bitch, Fascist."

"Somebody from your village?" Marson said.

"*Collaborazionista fascista bastardo.* Bastard."

"Yeah," Marson said. "Bastard."

Ridiculously, a memory came to him then of being in a high school class, at St. Anthony High School in Washington, D.C., in 1933, Sister Theresa's class in Shakespeare, and the play was *King Lear*. Students were asked to choose a passage to read aloud, and Marson had chosen the speech of Edmund's that ends with the phrase "stand up for bastards." Marson had spoken the phrase with such satisfaction and such gusto that the gentle nun had taken him aside after the class to explain the problem of enjoying life's inconsistencies too much. She had used the word. He had not understood, although he knew perfectly well that she did not like the way he had said the speech.

He lowered the carbine and nodded at the old man.

"'Stand up for bastards,'" he said. He felt something of himself coming back, and it frightened him, as if his mind would not be able to support it. He did not want to think of home now, or of love, or of family, hearth, hope, or a sleep that presumed that what you left for the province of dreams would be there when you came back. He helped Joyner get Asch up onto his shoulders, and the three of them headed down again, going faster now. The way was so steep that several times they had to get down and edge along, pulling Asch with them. Marson offered to take his own turn carrying him. But Joyner refused. Asch did not utter a sound, and his breathing had grown very shallow. The clouds over the moon thickened, and the rain started again, pellets at first, tiny pieces of hail, turning to water. "Christ, no," Joyner said. "Christ Almighty no. Fuck'n *rain.*"

The snow surface, already crusted over, became slick. They could still break through it, but it was so hard now that at times they slipped on it, and the breaking through would come from falling.

They came to the last steep part of the climb, the rock ledge where they had slept a little on the way up. They settled Asch in the lee of it and got down themselves, side by side— Joyner, Marson, and the old man. Here they were again, huddled out of the rain.

"An Italian," Marson said. "I can't figure it."

"They *were* on the other side," Joyner said. "Remember?"

"I'm sick."

Joyner said nothing.

Asch stirred and moaned. He opened his eyes and stared out. For an instant, Marson thought he might be dead. "Where are we?"

"Almost there," Marson said.

"I'm dead. I can feel the blood going out of me."

"You're imagining it."

"No."

"You are. It's your imagination."

"I have no imagination anymore," Asch said. "I'm all facts. That's me, Robert. Ask me anything." He sobbed. "Ask me if I'm gonna die."

"You'll make it. We're almost there. Save your strength. You *will* make it."

"Did you go to the serials?" Asch said. "Back home? The movie houses?"

Marson thought the other might be raving again. "Yes," he said.

"Saturday matinee," Asch said. "Remember?" He coughed—it seemed harmless, small, not connected to his wounds. He cleared his throat. "All day for a nickel."

"Yep."

"I always hated having to wait to see how it would turn out."

"Last-minute rescues," Joyner said.

"Right." Asch sobbed. "Goddamn it. I should've been in synagogue."

"Hey," Joyner said. "Marson got the son of a bitch that shot you, Saul."

"Well, then the son of a bitch and I will both be dead. *B'rikh hu.* You know what that means? That means 'Blessed is he.'"

"You'll be dead someday, like all of us," Joyner told him. "But first you're gonna be out of the fuck'n war."

"I wish I was Catholic sometimes."

"I wish I was Jewish sometimes," Marson said. He felt wrong, as if he had not taken the other man seriously enough.

"I could make my confession and be happy." So it was one of Asch's jokes.

"Don't know where we'll get our hands on a priest," Marson said.

"Can't any Catholic hear it?"

"Only baptism can be done by any Catholic."

"Okay, can I be baptized?"

"Do you really want to be?"

"Might as well cover all the bases." Asch smiled. "I never believed it much. We learned the prayers. Grew up with it."

"Hey," Joyner said. "Keep still and we'll get you down this fuck'n mountain and I'll baptize you myself."

"I'm a sinner."

"We all are," said Joyner.

"You carried me, Benny." Asch was weeping again. "I'm sorry. I'm sorry, Benny."

"I'm sorry, too. You're a heavy stinking bastard."

"I am."

"You're gonna remember saying all this when you're healed up and you're gonna be embarrassed, buddy."

"I wish I could've *savored* things more."

"Well, save your breath."

After a moment, Asch choked up something and spit. He said, "Is that blood?"

They did not answer him at first.

"Fellas?"

"It's too dark to see, okay?" Joyner said.

"Is it raining *again*?"

"Like the end of the fucking world," Marson told him.

TWENTY-FOUR

FINALLY, THEY STARTED DOWN AGAIN, churning up the crusted snow, once more being thrashed by the rain, which was needle thin, like tiny blades of ice. Joyner, carrying Asch, fell and slid with him in the breaking-up icy melting of the snow, and Marson had to help them both move from the base of the tree that had stopped their descent. The old man was making his way down ahead of them, carrying Asch's pack.

"Saul?" Joyner said, lifting him again. "Can you see his face?" he asked Marson, who could not. "You pissed on me, Asch. Hey, Asch."

"We're almost down," Marson said.

They came at last out onto the road, where they found that a tank battalion had come up. Joyner began to try to run. "He's not breathing," he said. "Goddamn it. I think he stopped breathing." They crossed the road. Joyner set Asch down on the bed of one of the two-and-a-half-ton trucks, and a corpsman with wide, heavy wrists and sloping shoulders walked over and took Asch's pulse. He blew into the mouth and pressed the chest, and then repeated this. He hit Asch's chest three times and put the side of his head down on the breastbone. At last he straightened. "Gone," he said. He reached into the wet shirt and ripped the dog tags off, put one into Asch's mouth, and punched the chin, so that it caught between the teeth. Joyner flew at him. "You fucking stupid son of a bitch!" he said, flailing. It took two of the others to subdue him. Joyner sat weeping on the ground with his arms draped over his upraised knees, the rain splattering off his helmet and his shoulders. The others stood around watching. Marson had sunk to the ground at the wheel of a jeep that had come up. He watched two soldiers carry Asch's body away. He could not find it in himself to feel anything. It was all death. Death, death. The rain kept coming down and the others walked away from Joyner, who could not stop. Joyner's voice went off into the predawn and the rain, the rushing of the river a few yards away through the trees.

The patrol had gone on. Skirmishers had come through the trees on the other side of the river. Glick was dead. McCaig and Lockhart were casualties, already invalided out of the war.

Overnight.

A captain, tall and dark blue eyed, with wire-framed eyeglasses, walked over and looked at them. "Fuck," he said. "This whole thing's fucked. What a royal fuckup."

Angelo stood near Corporal Marson, looking guilty, almost skulking, hands tucked into the front of his cloak. He was someone awaiting release. It was evident how little any of this meant to him. Marson resented him for it. He looked for the cart and the horse, the old man's earthly goods. It was like searching for some sign of sane, livable existence.

Joyner kept shaking his head and weeping, and when the captain stood over him he looked up, his face running with the rain and his tears. "Murderers," he said.

The captain said, "Yeah. Outstanding."

"Murderers," Joyner said.

The captain turned to a couple of the others. "Get him out of here, will you?"

They took Joyner by the arms, lifting him. Marson didn't know any of them. It was as if he had left one war and come back into another.

"I'm reporting it all," Joyner said.

The others half carried, half dragged him away. The captain walked over to Corporal Marson, who stood to face him. "You wanna tell me about this?"

"He's exhausted, sir," Marson said. "He carried Private Asch most of the way down this mountain."

"You get a view of what's down the road north?"

"An orderly retreat," Marson said emptily. "A big force, moving north."

"Tell me the rest of it."

He heard himself telling about the climb, the exhaustion, the dead soldier, the sniper who was not a German skirmisher

but an Italian straggler. While he told it all, Angelo stood waiting to be let go. He kept murmuring something, looking at the
other soldiers, blinking in the rain.

The captain glanced at him. "Search the old man," he said
to two others.

They took Angelo aside and went through his cloak. They
found the little bottle of schnapps, a few coins—and a drawn
map of this part of the country. The map showed positions of
American units in the area. "He's a spy," the captain said.
"Take him into the woods by the river and shoot him."

"What?" Marson said. "*What?*"

"You heard me."

"No, sir."

"Are you questioning me?"

"Sir—you can't mean it."

"Two soldiers in this outfit were shot by an SS officer and
his whore. Four others got it last night. From Italians—acting
like people happy to be liberated. You lost somebody from the
same actions. Some of them are still in this, and this one's carrying around scouting information on us. I'm not taking any
chances."

"He had nothing to do with this, sir."

"That's an order, Corporal. These people know the penalty
for spying."

"But he helped us get where we needed to, sir. He kept his
word."

"Yeah, and if they overrun us today, he'll go back to helping
them scout *us*. This patrol got the shit shot out of it this

morning, Corporal. They got it from a couple of peasants who looked just like him. Take care of it."

"But he isn't with them, sir. He's not with them." As Marson spoke the words he was not certain that they were true. He was not certain of anything.

"Look. You gonna do it, or will I?"

Angelo evidently realized what they were talking about. He began a low muttering and a kind of nervous dance, looking into the raining sky. "*Ave Maria,*" he said, loud, "*piena di grazia, il Signore è con te.*" His voice grew still louder as the captain turned to him, and Marson realized, through the second strand of pleading words, that he was saying the Hail Mary in his native language: "*Tu sei benedetta fra le donne e benedetto . . .*"

"Sir," Marson said. "Don't do this."

The captain unholstered his pistol.

"Wait, sir," Marson said. "He's my prisoner."

The captain stopped and looked at him. Others were watching as well. The old man looked around himself, at the soldiers standing there staring at him, and he said his prayer louder, dancing in pure terror. "*Ave Maria, piena di grazia . . .*"

Marson said again, "He's my prisoner, sir."

In the next moment, the old man's bladder emptied out— the urine ran down his legs and steamed at his feet. Marson looked at the rope-soled shoes.

"Take him over into the trees and do it," the captain said. "Now."

Corporal Marson leveled his carbine at Angelo and gestured for him to move off. The old man sank to his knees, crying, folding his hands, as if Marson were an icon to which he was praying.

"Get up," Marson said, aware of the others watching him.

The old man slowly got to his feet, still with hands clasped, looking at Marson with a mixture of disbelief and fright. "*Amico*," he pleaded. "Friend."

Marson gestured for him to walk ahead, and he began to move off in a mincing stride, weeping and saying the prayer. Corporal Marson knew the prayer well enough to repeat it with him, except that he could not recall the English. It was as if the words had never been in any other language.

They went into the trees on the river side of the road, and on down a path to the edge of the water. Marson kept gesturing for him to continue along the path, which wound away from the road. Dawn was breaking behind the heavy clouds, the sky turning to light, gray and cold, with black tatters drifting in it, and the freezing rain, still coming down, as if it had never stopped. Marson looked over his shoulder to see that he was out of sight of the road, and of the others. "Okay, hold it," he said to the old man. "Wait." Angelo stopped and turned, and now seemed to have gathered himself. There was something different about his eyes. Suddenly he said, "Pig," his mouth with its bad teeth open, his face fixed in a strange, gaping scowl.

Marson stared. The black eyes showed nothing. But then for an instant it was as if the old face had tightened with hatred.

"*Santa Maria, Madre di Dio, prega per noi peccatori, adesso e nell'ora della nostra morte. Amen.*"

"*Madre di Dio,*" Marson said to him.

Angelo sank to his knees. And in his face now you could see that he had nothing but loathing for the other, his expression defiant but resigned. There was an unnatural glitter of triumph in it, the look of someone who has proved himself right about something. Clearly he expected to die, and he had accepted it.

He had taken Marson and the others across the mountain because it was a way to survive, and Joyner had been right about him all along.

"Fascist," Marson said.

"*Uccidami,*" Angelo muttered through his teeth.

"I don't understand. No *capeesh.*"

"*Faccialo!*"

"No *capeesh.*"

"Do! Shoot. *Ti maledico!*"

Corporal Marson raised the barrel of the carbine, leveling it at the other's middle.

"*Maledico?*" he said.

"Visit hell," Angelo said.

"You're telling me to go to hell."

"*È bene che l'ebreo è morto.*"

"I think I understand you," Marson said. He wanted to shoot now. He felt the nerve pulse travel along his wrist to his finger on the trigger.

"Is a-good the Jew die."

He aimed the rifle. "Yeah," he said. "Pig."

"Prega per noi peccatori, adesso e nell'ora della nostra morte. Amen." The old man was talking fast now, eyes wide and frantic and full of hate.

Marson understood that the other had begun to pray again, and he paused once more. "You visited Washington, D.C."

"Che cosa." The old man muttered the words, head bowed, trying to master himself.

"You saw New York," Marson said.

"New York, *sì.* Washington." Something like expectation showed in the eyes. "I like."

"Catholic."

"Sì."

"You."

The old eyes gave back nothing. Marson stared at him, and had a moment when he thought they might begin to speak back and forth in some other language. Something passed between them, a kind of silent acknowledgment of what all of this had been, and the old man was indeed Catholic. And a Fascist, too.

"Fascist," Marson said.

And then again the praying began. *"Madre di Dio . . ."*

He looked back once more in the direction of the road, then turned and let the barrel of the carbine down. *"Via,"* he said. "Just go. Get the hell away from me."

Angelo looked at him. The dark eyes were unreadable now. Water ran down the lined face. He did not move. He went on muttering the prayer.

"Get out," Marson said. "Go. Run."

"*Santa Maria, Madre di Dio . . .*"

"Goddamn it," Marson said, low. "*Via! Via!*"

The old man stood slowly, feebly, the legs barely holding him up, face contorted with his defiance and with the certainty that he was about to die. But then he began pleading again for his life, crying and holding out his skeletal hands. Marson felt a sudden black surge of rage, a kind of revulsion at the other's abjectness, given what he was, the pitiful shape of him there, the dark eyes pleading, and the centuries-old hatreds in him, the crying, going on, rain and tears on the old face with its high twin networks of wrinkles over the eyes. Marson, in his exhaustion and his emptiness, raised the barrel of the carbine, and said, once more, "*Via.*" He experienced another urge to shoot, go ahead and do it now. Do it. It would only be another Fascist. It might as well be the devil himself.

The old man turned, took a step, and then fell to his knees.

Marson walked over and put the barrel of the carbine against the base of his skull. He had been ordered to do this. The old man kept praying, and again Marson said, "Goddamn you. *Via! Via!*" He reached down and took hold of the cloak, and pulled him to his feet. Then he made a gesture, waving him away, and he fired the rifle into the wet earth. One shot. The old man jumped, and fell to the ground again, covering his face. Marson felt an overwhelming desire to be rid of him, and now he, too, was weeping. "*Via*, goddamn you. Go. Go."

At last, Angelo seemed to understand. Weeping, bowing, he got to his feet and started backing away, and he was nothing more than an old man who had tried to use both sides to go on being who he had ignorantly been all his long life. He went along the path, and around that bend of the river, still looking back, still saying the prayer. Marson sat down in the middle of the path and, laying the rifle across his knees, put his hands to his face. "Hail Mary," he said, "full of grace. The Lord is with thee." But he could not find the rest of the words.

He wept a little, thinking of what he had come near to doing, and of what he had already done, and thinking, too, of Asch and the others. Asch was dead. And Glick was dead, too. The war had got him. There was nothing to report, now, nothing to say or do about all that. He looked where the old man had gone. Angelo, the Fascist, had survived the night. Angelo would say or be anything to survive. He was an old man in a war, on the losing side. And Robert Marson had let him go. There was not much a seventy-year-old Italian man would be able to do to change the war. And maybe something or someone else would kill him, but Robert Marson of 1236 Kearney Street in Washington, D.C., had not done so.

Morning had come, light spreading across the low sky. The corporal got to his feet and started back toward the road. Just before he reached sight of it, and the others, he stopped, feeling something rise in him. The rain was increasing. The wind had died. The clouds were showing places where sun might come through, or it might not. There was no sound of firing, and the river ran with its steady roar. He waited, breathing slowly.

It was peace. It was the world itself, water rushing near the lip of the bank from the storms, the snow and the winter rain. He felt almost good, here. He thought of home, and he could see it, that street, those people. He had found a way back to imagining it. For a few moments, he believed that he might simply stay here by this river. He wanted to. It came to him that he had never wanted anything so much. It would be perfectly simple. He would lie down and let the war go on without him, and when it was over and the killings had stopped, he would get up and go home. He thought of going off in the direction the old man had taken, of finding some-place away. Someplace far.

He turned in a small circle and looked at the grass, the rocks, the river, the raining sky with its ragged and torn places, the shining bark of the wet trees all around. He could not think of any prayers now. But every movement felt like a kind of adoration.

Then the feeling dissolved, was gone, like a breath.

His foot hurt. It was probably infected. He turned his face up into the rain and sobbed, once, like a gasp, and then it was as if he were letting go a silent scream, standing there shaking, frozen in the attitude of the scream, head turned to the sky, mouth open. No sound came. There was just the tremor, the tensed muscles, the eyes shut tight, the mouth open. The rain hit his face, and when the muscles of his jaw relaxed, he kept his mouth wide, and drank. He could not believe how thirsty he had become. He let his mouth fill with the rain, then swal-lowed. It was so cold. He let it fill, and swallowed again. He took one more look around himself. A pattern of the water had formed in a wild tangle of a thicket, a silver shimmer dropping onto the mud of the path. The water was so clear and clean.

He shouldered his carbine and made his way back into the war.

This is Richard Bausch's eleventh novel. He is also the author of seven volumes of short stories. His work has appeared in the *New Yorker, Atlantic Monthly, Esquire, Playboy, GQ, Harper's Magazine*, and other publications and has been featured in numerous best-of collections, including *O. Henry Prize Stories, Best American Short Stories*, and *New Stories from the South*. In 2004 he won the PEN/Malamud Award for Short Fiction. He is Chancellor of the Fellowship of Southern Writers and lives in Memphis, Tennessee, where he is Moss Chair of Excellence in the Writer's Workshop of the University of Memphis.

A NOTE ON THE TYPE

This book was set in Caledonia, a typeface designed by W. A. Dwiggins (1880–1956). It belongs to the family of printing types called "modern face" by printers – a term used to mark the change in style of the type letters that occurred around 1800. Caledonia borders on the general design of Scotch Roman but it is more freely drawn than that letter. This version of Caledonia was adapted by David Berlow in 1979.